Carol
OF THE ROOMS

ENDORSEMENTS

Carol of the Rooms is a delightful new take on Dickens's *A Christmas Carol*. Diana Leagh Matthews has cleverly woven a musical theme into this modern retelling, which introduces readers to the soundtrack of Terri Neely's life. *Carol of the Rooms* is set to be a new holiday favorite.
—**Heidi Glick**, Author of *Dog Tags* and *Hold for Release*

Diana Leagh Matthews has captured the essence of the Christmas story—God's Christmas story—in her version of Dickens's *A Christmas Carol*. It's not hard to imagine the circumstances that created a Scrooge spirit in Terri Neely's life or the level of hurt to overcome as she faced her own demons. Leagh expertly draws the reader in to experience God's story of extravagant love and forgiveness. Don't wait for Christmas to indulge in this wonderful tale!
—**Sally Ferguson**, Reviewer, Caregiver, Encourager & Author of *How to Plan a Women's Retreat Playbook*

In *Carol of the Rooms*, Diana Leagh Matthews has crafted an entertaining modern-day retelling of *A Christmas Carol* in which Terri Neely is taken on a journey to her past, present, and future, exposing her selfish ambitions and the reasons she lost her love of music. The author has done an excellent job of showing the reader how a life can be transformed when putting God and family first.
—**Andrea Merrell**, Professional Freelance Editor and Author of *Murder of a Manuscript*, *Marriage: Make It or Break It*, and *Praying for the Prodigal*

In this modern-day interpretation of *A Christmas Carol*, Terri Neely is a businesswoman with a painful past who has

dedicated her life to money, success, and power. Author Diana Leagh Matthews deftly and cleverly weaves music, spiritual messages, and imagination throughout this tale, allowing the story and its powerful message of love to gently unfold. Readers are sure to be changed by this new spin on a timeless story.
—**Chris Posti**, Award-winning author of novels for women over 50

Ms. Matthews has crafted a touching story inspired by Dickens's *A Christmas Carol*. Combining that traditional tale with a near-death experience, angels, and multi-generational characters, she has woven the music of our lives into her story, giving it an added depth that inspires and encourages.
—**Bettie Boswell**, Author of Christian romances *On Cue*, *Free to Love*, and *Hoping for Treasure* and Christian children's books *Lucy and Thunder* and *Dottie's Dream Horse*

How is it possible for *Carol of the Rooms* to move from serious, sad, and daunting, to grace- and faith-filled, redeeming, and joyful? This work of fiction rings with the truth of a familiar storyline that brings the Lord and the plans He has for each of us into focus. We can see our own struggles. Yet the joy and hope and love of God come shining through. Wonderfully written, full of grace, *Carol of the Rooms* is a story to cherish.
—**Helen Baratta**, Author, Speaker, and Director of Development for First Place for Health

"What's not to love about a modern retelling of *A Christmas Carol*? Diana Leagh Matthews weaves the classic story together with biblical truths in a truly unique way."
–**Karin Beery**, author of hopeful fiction with a healthy dose of romance

Carol
OF THE ROOMS

Diana Leagh Matthews

A Christian Company
ElkLakePublishingInc.com

COPYRIGHT NOTICE

Carol of the Rooms
First edition. Copyright © 2023 by Diana Leagh Matthews. The information contained in this book is the intellectual property of Diana Leagh Matthews and is governed by United States and International copyright laws. All rights reserved. No part of this publication, either text or image, may be used for any purpose other than personal use. Therefore, reproduction, modification, storage in a retrieval system, or retransmission, in any form or by any means, electronic, mechanical, or otherwise, for reasons other than personal use, except for brief quotations for reviews or articles and promotions, is strictly prohibited without prior written permission by the publisher.

This is a work of fiction. Names, characters, businesses, places, events, locales, and incidents are either the products of the author's imagination or used in a fictitious manner. Any resemblance to actual persons, living or dead, or actual events is purely coincidental.

Cover and Interior Design: Kelly Artieri, Deb Haggerty
Editor(s): Kristin Cooney, Cristel Phelps, Deb Haggerty

PUBLISHED BY: Elk Lake Publishing, Inc., 35 Dogwood Drive, Plymouth, MA 02360, 2023

Library Cataloging Data
Names: Matthews, Diana Leagh (Diana Leagh Matthews)
Carol of the Rooms / Diana Leagh Matthews

250 p. 23cm × 15cm (9in × 6 in.)
ISBN-13: 9798891340862 (paperback) | 9798891340879 (trade paperback) | 9798891340886 (e-book)
Key Words: Holiday Fiction; Christian Women's Fiction; Contemporary Fiction; Family Life Fiction; Christian Contemporary Fiction; Christian Fantasy; Religious Literature & Fiction
Library of Congress Control Number: 2023948154 Fiction

DEDICATIONS

This book is dedicated to my three daddies.

First, to my earthly daddy, Rev. Clarence Allen. You instilled the foundation for the soundtrack of my life, sowing a love of music and God's Word into my heart. From the beginning, you taught me about both of these. Words can't thank you enough for sharing these truths with me. I miss you more than words can ever say. I also miss performing with you and look forward to the day we can sing and praise God together again.

Secondly, to Daddy Rabbit, Rev. Herbert Neely. I only knew you the last year of your life but will never forget you. You taught me, regardless of our situation or condition, that the soundtrack of our lives remains within us. Sometimes we just have to look for it a little harder or express the melody within us in other ways.

Last, but definitely not least, to my heavenly Father and my Lord and Savior. Thank You for offering me the best gift in the world, salvation. I am blessed You allow me to share the soundtrack of my life through word and song.

ACKNOWLEDGMENTS

Writing a book is a labor of love and a lot of hard work. This book would not be possible without the help of so many people in the years it's taken to raise this book child into reality.

Holding this book in my hands after almost a decade of work feels very surreal and brings a mix of emotions: awe and joy, a little trepidation, disbelief it is finally a reality, and hope for what the Lord has in store.

My greatest prayer is all who read this book will be blessed. I want to thank each of the following people or groups for their invaluable help:

My Word Weavers Page 12 group for being the first to see this story and stretching me to make it even better. I couldn't have done this without you: Anna Grace Miller, Kass Fogle, Martha Hyman, and Paige Snedeker. You each pushed and challenged me to make the story the best it possibly could be.

Cynthia Ruchti for looking over the early drafts and providing me with invaluable feedback to improve those first few chapters.

Andrea Merrill for helping me polish the rough edges and getting the story ready to submit for publication.

Theresa Patten for providing guidance and feedback on cerebral palsy.

My brother, Rev. Dr. Lane Allen, for answering my theology and Bible questions.

E.V. Sparrow and Tamelia Aday for walking the journey toward publication alongside me and serving as a sounding board at times.

My WordMama, Kathy Carlton Willis, and dear friend and mentor, Dee Dee Parker, for pushing me out of my comfort zone and for constantly encouraging me more times than I can count. I would never have made it to this point without both of you.

My dear prayer team for your prayers and encouragement over the years. It's been a long journey to get to this point, and your prayers kept me going.

Deb Haggerty and her team at Elk Lake Publishing for your patience in walking with me each step of the way toward publication. A special thank you to Kristin Cooney for helping me mine the hidden gemstones.

My family for listening to me brainstorm and discuss characters even when they had no idea whom or what I was talking about. Thank you for being there and allowing me the time to write.

And to God Almighty for making this book possible. This book would not be here without Your guidance. May You be given all the honor and glory in this story.

CHAPTER 1

Dead. At least that's the way Terri Neely felt. Her heart had died long ago—which was exactly how she preferred to live her life. Self-preservation had become her new motto. And she would stop at nothing to protect herself from ever being hurt again.

Terri logged into her online bank account. Time to review the balance. She checked her account multiple times a day and loved the way her heart fluttered each time the numbers increased. Sometimes, she would make a large withdrawal just for the feel of all those wonderful crisp bills in her hand. Her mouth salivated at the memory.

Marlee Jacobson, her mentor, often said, "You can't ever have too much money." Terri had adopted her friend's attitude.

She glanced at the date on the bottom right of her computer: November 22, 2006. One year ago today, Marlee died.

Terri had visited her mentor and friend around appointments at their architectural firm every day as Marlee valiantly fought cancer. Terri looked at the portrait on the wall where the familiar blonde hair cascaded around narrow shoulders.

Her hand went to her mouth. *Did Marlee's eyes move?* She stood and walked over to the picture, then swallowed. Hard. *I must be losing it.*

Sea-green eyes glistened back at her. The blonde hair glowed.

Terri opened her mouth and closed it. She took a step closer and studied the portrait. It had been so difficult to watch her friend slowly wither away. Although sick, no one expected she'd actually die. Who would have ever imagined she'd be gone at fifty-three—only a decade older than Terri.

When Marlee flatlined, Terri felt as if the air had been sucked out of her lungs, but her friend came back and lingered for three more days. Talking had been difficult, but she had asked to see Gramps.

Thoughts of Terri's beloved grandfather brought a smile.

The woman in the picture suddenly spoke. "There's so much I wanted to tell you back then but couldn't."

Terri jumped back. "What?" She blinked, then squeezed her eyes shut. *Can grief really do this to someone?* She looked back at the image on the wall.

The image smiled. "No, I'm really here. Now I can say what I couldn't then."

Okay, I'll play along. "Such as?" Terri clenched her hands as her heart thudded against her chest. *Maybe I need some serious medication.*

"I was wrong. There's so much more to life than money. I don't want you to end up like me." A rattling sound filled the room. "My chains are heavy. I can't change my fate, but you can change yours."

Terri crossed her arms and shuddered as the chains continued to rattle. "What fate?"

Carol OF THE ROOMS

"Do you remember when I came back?"

A memory flashed of the doctor and nurses rushing around while Terri stood back helplessly. They had revived Marlee, who lingered for three more days. Terri had been confident her friend would make a full recovery. "Of course."

"I tried to tell you." Marlee sighed. "You wouldn't listen."

"And I don't have to stay now—" Terri turned toward her office door, but her feet wouldn't budge.

"An angel appeared to me and told me I had a choice. He showed me two extremes."

Terri clenched her jaw. She refused to face the picture but could see it from the corner of her eye.

"The first place he took me was dark and menacing. People screamed in pain. They were captives of their own making. Fire burned hotter than anything I've ever felt before."

A sarcastic laugh escaped as Terri turned back to her friend. "Apparently, they've never been in Charlotte when it's a hundred and five degrees and humid."

"You don't get it." The green eyes filled with frustration. "I was in Hell."

"That's only a fairy tale." Terri rocked back on her heels. "I should know. I've heard the stories enough." She thought of her beloved evangelist grandfather and her father following in his footsteps. But that was before—

"Hell is no fairy tale. It's real." Marlee's nose flared.

Terri ran a hand over the back of her neck. "And the second place?"

Her friend's face now held an afterglow. "Beautiful is an understatement. Light is everywhere. I've never seen colors so vibrant and beautiful. Flowers with colors we've never imagined. Waterfalls glisten, and streams dot the landscape. And the music ... oh, the music."

"That's enough!" Terri roared.

"Let me finish," Marlee insisted. "The music was melodious and serene. All around, people sang praises to God. And I saw Him, Terri. I saw Jesus. His eyes held nothing but kindness and love. I've never experienced such peace, love, and compassion before."

"You imagined things." How many times had her mentor told her that over the years? She'd never had any interest in God before.

"No, I didn't." Certainty shone in those green eyes. "My grandmother and aunt were there. I believe—"

"You believe what?" Terri's voice held more sarcasm than she intended.

"I believe I saw your parents. At least, they looked like the pictures I've seen of them."

Terri's back stiffened, and she tried again to walk away. "I don't want to hear it."

A huge sigh came from the photo. "I know, but you've got to. In those three days I lingered, your Gramps told me about Jesus and helped me make peace with Him." A tear slid down her cheek.

"Good for you. God's not done a thing for me but allow heartache." Her whole life had been full of pain, loss, and misery. Where had serving God gotten her parents?

"Oh, my friend. He loves you more than you know." Marlee's voice choked with emotion. "We've both been wrong. I made peace, but it's almost too late for you. God wants you to know He's going to do whatever it takes to get your attention."

Terri rolled her eyes.

Chains rattled and then crashed. "Now that I've made things right with God and told you of His truth, my chains are gone. It's time for you to lose yours. I'll be praying for you." Another long sigh escaped the picture as it returned to normal.

Terri screamed. Her knees threatened to buckle.

Her assistant ran into the room. "Miss Neely? Are you okay?"

Terri stared first at the picture, then at Abigail. "Sorry. Just my imagination running wild."

It was, wasn't it? What if what I heard is true?

An hour later—after convincing herself stress had made her imagine the encounter with Marlee—Terri picked up the stack of pictures she'd developed that morning and flipped through the ones of the high-rise condominiums. Victoria Nelson was her interior designer on this multi-million-dollar project.

While flipping through the photos, Terri stopped and stared in disbelief. She had been specific about what she expected for the design of the apartment. There should be a black leather couch with a matching recliner and glass table.

Instead, Victoria had completely changed the design and aesthetics. The room contained a modern two-piece taupe sectional with a cocktail ottoman and wall mirror over an end table.

"This will never do." She threw the pictures on her desk. This was the third time she'd worked with Victoria. The designer always strove to please her in the past, but this time the woman had gone completely against her wishes.

Terri considered her options. She could call Victoria, demand she change the room back to her original request, or she could ask why Victoria had completely gone against her wishes.

Marlee came back to mind. Her words about heaven and hell crowded Terri's brain. She shook her head to erase them. *I have to forget that silly fantasy.*

Abigail buzzed her. "Mr. Peterson called. He needs to reschedule his appointment for tomorrow."

The announcement produced a scowl. "Did he have a good reason?"

Abigail cleared her throat. "They rushed his mother-in-law to the hospital this morning."

Terri waved her hand. "Fine. I'll see him then." She hung up, picked up the pictures again, stared at them, then threw them back down. "That's it." She would not allow a simple interior designer to run over her—even if Victoria *was* a famous, award-winning designer.

"No one crosses me."

A few simple strokes revealed the necessary phone number. Terri called the Better Business Bureau. "Yes, I need to file a complaint." It didn't matter that Victoria was the top interior designer in *all* the Southeast. The time had come for this woman to learn you do not cross Terri Neely.

CHAPTER 2

Terri stormed into her grandfather's house the following afternoon. Gramps sat in his chair with his eyes closed, snoring softly. Thankfully, his fall had caused no harm.

She searched for her father's sisters.

"Why didn't you call me sooner?" Terri yelled at her aunts once she walked into the kitchen. Didn't they realize how serious a fall could be for a man his age?

Aunt Maggie looked up from her place at the table, her eyes filled with weariness. "Nothing to tell."

Aunt Beth brushed too-long bangs from her eyes. "He needs to be in a nursing home." She'd been telling them for over a year that Gramps would receive better care in a facility than at home.

"No, he doesn't." Terri clenched her fists. "They won't give him the care he needs." She'd been emphatic he stay at home, refusing to ship him off to a nursing home where he'd be just another patient. He needed to be with people who loved and cared about him.

"They are very attentive. Not only will he have the medical care needed, but he'll have friends to talk with." Aunt Beth had toured various nursing facilities in Charlotte for the past four months. She'd become a mini expert on all the amenities these places claimed to offer.

Terri paced back and forth. "He could fall, and they might not know it for hours."

"That could happen here." Maggie's voice held a hint of irritation.

"That's why we have that medical alert thing." Why couldn't they understand how important it was for her to have him here? Gramps and this house were her last links to her parents.

"I'm glad we were here when he fell." Beth had been at her father's side within seconds, his health of great concern to both sisters. Gramps had given Terri, his oldest grandchild, both financial and medical power of attorney. Gramps had a soft spot for his son's only child, plus she was very business savvy and understood his wishes. Sentiment would not impede her decision-making process the way it would his daughters.

Ethan Brown strolled into the kitchen at that moment. "He'll be fine."

Terri stared at Gramps's nurse who visited three times a week, glad she had hired him from a nearby home health agency. There was nothing she wouldn't do for her grandfather.

"Are you sure?" Terri chewed on her bottom lip. Gramps meant the world to her. He was the only person who loved her and whom she loved in return. The only person who had ever been there for her.

"I'm positive. He has no broken bones. I gave him a good physical. I also checked his blood pressure. It's normal."

"What about his blood sugar?" Gramps loved his sweets, but his sugar often shot up, although a prescription helped to keep his levels even.

Ethan opened the freezer and pulled out a sugar-free treat. "His sugar's fine. Actually, he's cracking jokes and sent me in here to ask for an ice cream bar."

"I think he wanted you to spy on us." Beth's shoulders relaxed, her tone more jovial than it was a moment earlier.

"What are you talking about in there?" Gramps called from his recliner in the living room, the place where he spent most of his days.

Terri took the treat from Ethan and walked into the living room. "The scare you gave us." She leaned over and kissed the top of his head.

"I'm fine." Gramps gave her a sly grin.

She recognized that look and knew he had something on his mind. "What are you up to now?"

"Oh, nothing." He seemed too happy considering the ordeal he had gone through earlier. "How was your day?"

Terri sat in the recliner next to Gramps chair. The two had a good chat while her aunts stayed in the kitchen. Exactly how she preferred things. Gramps all to herself. She hated having to share her time with him and had not changed her mind about wanting him all to herself for years.

Ethan returned from the kitchen. "He's been telling me about his travels."

"Gramps has traveled the world." She had accompanied him on many of those trips while growing up and relished every memory.

"That's what he said. I think it's wonderful he's taken the Word of God to so many people."

Terri sat on her hands and pursed her lips. Her eyes slammed shut as her recent encounter with Marlee came to mind.

"He even sang for me ..." Ethan apparently tried to fill the awkward silence. "Sing it again, sir."

"I sing because I'm happy," Gramps belted out as he turned to her. "You used to love this one. Sing with me."

Terri crossed her arms and remained silent.

"I sing because I'm free," Ethan added, looking at her with anticipation.

"For his eye is on the sparrow ..." Gramps held out a hand.

"And he *used* to watch over me." Her voice held no emotion as she handed Gramps the remote.

Sadness dimmed his eyes. Taking her cue, he turned the TV on. "Look, I didn't know he was on now." Gramps turned up the volume.

Terri recognized the preacher. She'd heard him preach often, and he'd even been to the house to visit with Gramps. "I've got to go." She walked over to Gramps and bent to kiss him again on the top of his head. That was her spot.

Everywhere she turned, God tried to remind her of his love. She didn't believe it any longer and had to get out of there.

"Okay." Gramps looked betrayed, but his voice held a tenderness she didn't understand. *Why are you running?* his big blue eyes seemed to shout.

When was the last time anyone looked at her in such a way?

Ethan appeared at her side. "I'll walk you out."

CHAPTER 3

"I'll be home as soon as I can." Abigail pictured her son on the other end of the telephone with his chestnut hair and baby-blue eyes.

"I miss you." His sweet voice made her heart sing.

She longed to pull six-year-old Timmy into her arms and hold him tight. "I miss you too, sweetheart." She cherished each moment they had together.

"Will you be able to tuck me in tonight?" His voice filled with longing. Bedtime had long been a favorite ritual for both of them. Although the day was only beginning, she looked forward to that precious time with her son. Too often, work commitments found her arriving home long after he'd gone to bed. Last night had been a perfect example, which was probably why he asked her about it this morning.

"I hope so." Her goal was to be home before Timmy's time for bed. The sixty-plus-hour work weeks she consistently put in for Miss Neely left her exhausted, but she had no choice. Timmy's medical bills continued to mount and overwhelm her. He remained her first and most important priority.

Timmy's voice broke into her thoughts. "Can you tell me a story?"

"Sure, what would you like to hear?" She thought for a moment. "Superman?" One of his favorites.

"No, tell me Peter Pan."

Abigail's heart dropped. *Again?*

"After all, he's the boy who can fly." His voice rang with laughter.

She whispered in an amused voice, "I believe he's your new favorite."

"He is. Do you know why?" Timmy asked in a high-pitched, melodic voice.

"Why?" Her son always made her smile. Abigail wished she could stare into those precious blue eyes.

"Because he believes he can do things no one else can."

"Just like you." Her heart broke over all her son had to endure. He'd been born with cerebral palsy and, even though he was six years old, still could not walk. He never let his disability get him down. She'd never met a sweeter child. If only she could afford the surgery on his legs. Then there would at least be a chance he'd walk.

"I can fly through the air ..." he sang to her.

She could picture those little arms stretched out in flight. "One day you will." *Please let me find a way to keep my promise, Lord.* She barely scraped by on the minimum wage Miss Neely paid her. That's why she accepted all the overtime available. Everything she earned went to pay Timmy's medical bills and provide him with the best possible care. She needed to research other options for help.

Keys jingled at the front door. Abigail kept the door locked when at the office alone.

"I've got to go," she whispered into the phone. "Tell Grandma I'll call her later, if possible." She thanked God for her parents. Abigail would never make it without them.

Carol OF THE ROOMS

She and Timmy lived in their basement apartment, and her parents looked after Timmy while she worked. Living with them had hurt in getting more assistance for Timmy's needs, though. Their income had been included with hers, and she'd been penalized.

"Okay, Mommy. I love you." He had the innocence only a child could possess.

"I love you too." The call ended as the door opened. "Good morning, Miss Neely," Abigail greeted her boss as she placed the phone in its cradle.

Terri's arms overflowed with design books, which she laid on a round table in the center of the room. "What's on the agenda for today?"

How typical of her not to return the greeting.

Abigail reviewed the schedule. "You have a meeting with Mr. Peterson at ten. Then you have a luncheon with Mr. Hamlin to discuss his new project."

Terri picked up the mail from her inbox. "Cancel that meeting."

"Would you like to reschedule?" Abigail flipped through the appointment book.

Terri stopped for a moment. "Only if he insists. I did some research into his plans. What he has in mind is substandard for our firm."

"Maybe you could help him develop a better—"

"This is *my* business. I'll run it the way I deem best." Terri headed toward her office.

"Yes, ma'am." Abigail never understood her boss's outbursts. Though used to them, she noticed they'd increased since the death of Miss Jacobson last year. She'd hoped Miss Neely was finally moving on in the grieving process, but ... oh yes, yesterday had been the anniversary of Miss Jacobson's death. Maybe that's what had set Miss Neely's nerves on edge.

Abigail stood and followed, referring to her notepad. "Victoria Nelson would like an appointment with you at your earliest convenience. I have her down for four o'clock—"

"Cancel the appointment," Terri barked over her shoulder.

"But she said it's important." Victoria had sounded frantic when she called.

Terri stood in her office doorway. "I know what it's about. I refuse to meet with her."

"But she keeps calling." Why was her boss being so difficult?

Terri swung around and stared at her assistant. "Then you deal with her, but if you put her through to me—" She peered down at Abigail, who shuddered at the intensity of the steely stare. Something dark and menacing filled her boss's eyes. "You're fired."

Terri's words sent a sucker punch to Abigail's stomach. A moment later, the office door slammed shut.

Picking up the phone, Abigail thought about when she started at the firm three years ago. Miss Neely and Miss Jacobson were both difficult women, but the surviving partner had hardened even more. When she hired Abigail, Miss Neely promised to teach her everything she knew about becoming an architect. Abigail had shared her dreams of working in the industry, and Miss Neely promised to mentor her and take her under her wing.

Finding this job had been a dream. Her husband had served in the United States Army in Afghanistan. After his death, Abigail hoped she'd be able to return to school. Timmy was three at the time, but his medical bills engulfed the paltry insurance left by his father. She put her dream on hold. Or so she thought until she began working at Jacobson and Neely Architects. When she took the job, she thought all her dreams were about to come true. If only she'd known she would become trapped in the daily grind Terri Neely set for herself.

CHAPTER 4

Terri switched through the different stations on her car radio. Maybe she'd find something she wanted to listen to, although doubtful. In her opinion, the radio played nothing but junk, and she had no interest in most of today's so-called popular music. After tuning in to various stations, she stopped the search when she heard a Chopin nocturne. She'd always been a fan of Chopin, especially after learning to play most of his nocturnes as a child. She allowed the music to soar through the car. Chopin lifted her mood.

Glancing up from her reverie, she slammed the brakes when a car ran a red light and came within an inch of hitting her. A string of profanity the likes of which would break Gramps's heart flowed from her mouth.

Deep breaths. She gritted her teeth, made her way through the intersection, and pushed another button on the radio.

One breath ... two breaths ...

Three deep breaths ...

That was close, but I'm going to be okay.

Angelic voices sang across the radio station airwaves. "Silent night, holy night. All is calm. All is bright."

What? She blinked in surprise at the Christmas carol. *I forgot it's the Christmas season. What a joke.* She changed the station.

"O little town of Bethlehem ..." Change.

"The first noel, the angels did say ..." Change.

"I. Don't. Want. To. Have. A. Merry. Christmas!" Terri bit out the words. Change.

"We won't have a white Christmas in Charlotte." Change.

"Jingle bells ..." Change. Change.

"Angels we have heard on high, sweetly singing o'er the—"

That's it. Terri turned the radio off. Nothing good on any of these stations.

Her mind drifted to the obligations of the day. Tomorrow would be Thanksgiving Day. For many businesses, today meant a partial workday, but she had no intention of closing early. She would be there all day. No need to miss out on a dollar less than could be earned. She'd signed a deal with Mr. Peterson to design a skyscraper for his international business moving to the area. That would pad her bank account nicely. Her heart leapt at the thought of all those bills in her hand.

Her smile dissipated when she pulled into the lot and parked. Waiting for her was the one person she didn't want to see. Ever.

She pushed open her car door. "What do you want?"

"Good to see you too, Aunt Ri," Emma said.

Her adopted niece stood before Terri for her annual visit. The girl grated on her nerves. She was always so sweet. Too sweet. Emma never gave up trying to include Terri in various holiday celebrations—no matter how much Terri wished she would.

"I hate that name." Terri bristled, grabbing her purse and files for the office.

Carol OF THE ROOMS

Emma seemed to ignore her aunt's sour mood. "Happy Thanksgiving."

"If you say so." Terri pulled her keys out of the ignition.

"Derrick and I want you to join us for Thanksgiving dinner."

"I'll pass." Terri stepped out of the car and shot the young woman a menacing look.

"But we'll have turkey, ham, macaroni and cheese, homemade dressing—"

"I said I'd pass." Terri slammed the car door and stormed toward her office building. "Don't follow me," she called over her shoulder. She had no desire to spend time with this girl. Why did Sophia ever make her Emma's godmother? Terri had no use for the young woman. After all, she'd lived while her mother died giving birth to her.

Terri caught her breath. *I miss my best friend.*

"If you change your mind, we'd love to have you," Emma called one last time.

That girl wouldn't give up.

Aunt Beth called later in the morning. "What are your Thanksgiving plans?"

Terri drummed her fingers on her desk, eager to get this conversation over with. "Gramps and I will spend it together."

"Maggie and I plan to bring our families over. We'll prepare all the food." Hope rang in her aunt's voice.

"Gramps and I will spend it *alone*," Terri blurted, emphasizing the last word.

"Now listen, we're his family as well." Her aunt's voice rose an octave.

Terri sighed in frustration. She'd been having the same conversation with her aunts and Emma for years. *I hate the holidays.* "I'll be there at three p.m. I expect everyone to be *gone*." She practically yelled the last word into the phone.

"You're not being fair!" Aunt Beth shouted, creating static over the line.

"You want to talk about fair?" Anger rose in Terri's voice with each word.

"Not again." Aunt Beth sighed in exasperation. "What about Christmas?"

"What about it?" Personally, she would be glad when it was over.

"Christmas is the celebration of the birth of our Savior."

Aunt Beth wasn't telling her anything she didn't already know. "Save it! I've heard it all before. It's just another day and cuts into my profits."

Her aunt repeated her popular phrase. "There's more to life than money."

"So I've been told." A soft knock sounded. Terri looked up to discover a woman dressed in a black sheath dress in the doorway. "I've got to go." Thankful for an excuse, she hung up on her aunt. Weary of another hard-luck story, she stood and forced her friendliest smile onto her face. "May I help you?"

"I'm May Patterson with St. Andrews Children's Home." The woman took a step inside Terri's office, hope shining in her eyes. "We're collecting donations to help our children. All donations will go to buy Christmas presents and clothes for them this holiday season." She looked as if she could use new clothes herself, her dress faded and worn.

"Why are you *here*?" Terri's tone came out as hard as a piece of steel.

Carol OF THE ROOMS

The woman's face still held a look of hope. "We were hoping you would help. After all, this is the Christmas season."

"Exactly what help do you need?" Terri sat back down. Hopefully, the woman would take the hint to leave.

"Well, the donations are a big help, but I have an even larger request."

"Then make it." She scooted back in her office chair, wanting the woman to see her disinterest.

The woman's hands shook. "We're ... we're outgrowing our space. I hear you're the best architect in town."

Terri's chest puffed out. "That's because I am."

May straightened her shoulders as if to summon courage. "Would you help us redesign our space? We've got to find some way to expand."

Could this woman be serious? "What is your budget?"

The woman's hands continued to shake. "We don't have one. I was hoping you would be kind enough to donate some time."

Terri gave a mocking laugh. "I do *not* donate my time. What about the donations you're collecting?" Her chair creaked as she sprang to her feet.

"That money is to help the children. This is the only way they can have clothes or even a toy to open on Christmas morning." The woman stopped, visibly fighting back tears. "It's Christmas. Please have a heart." She folded her hands in a begging gesture.

"Go find your handouts elsewhere. You won't find them here." Terri moved toward the woman, who took several steps backward until stepping into the main office.

"But they're children ..." May's voice filled with despair.

"I really don't care. I'm sure they can work for what they need. Don't you have chores or—"

"I'm sorry, Miss Neely." Abigail appeared from the storage room on the other side of the office. "Maybe I can help you," she said to the visitor.

Terri gave both women a steely glance before turning on her heels and walking back into her office. "To the door, Abigail. Only to the door." She would relish slamming the door in her visitor's face.

CHAPTER 5

"How was your Thanksgiving?" Ethan asked the next time they saw one another.

"Fine. Gramps and I were together." Terri patted her grandfather's hand.

"He told me." Ethan brushed a stray hair from his eyes. "He missed having the entire family together."

He needs to drop the subject. "I don't want to talk about it. How is his blood sugar?"

"Normal."

"Good." Gramps sat up straighter in his chair. "When can I have a donut?"

Terri couldn't help but grin. He always loved donuts, but since he'd become diabetic two years ago, she refused to let him have the delicacy.

"I'll see what I can do," Ethan promised with a smile—a smile that could win anyone over. Terri turned her head but not before her heart skipped a beat.

Gramps turned toward the young man beside him. "Sounds good. What did you do for Thanksgiving?"

"I spent the morning helping at the homeless shelter. So many come in who have nothing." He shook his head sadly and stared at the door before continuing. "I want to help those who are less fortunate. That evening, I went to my parents' home for dinner."

"Never married?"

Terri shot Gramps a warning glance.

"Divorced." Ethan did not look in her direction.

Terri squirmed in her seat. More than she cared to hear.

"Read any good books lately?" Ethan broke into her thoughts.

Did he sense her discomfort at the discussion of his marital status? "Right now, I'm reading a book about building a stronger business."

He looked amused. "Is that all you read? I mean, books on business?"

"Usually. From time to time, I'll read something else." For the next thirty minutes, the pair discussed their favorite authors.

"Your grandfather is a special man," Ethan told her as she walked him to the door.

They stepped outside, and she wrapped a shawl around her shoulders. "I think so." Thoughts of Gramps warmed her like nothing else.

"I've grown very fond of him. It's almost like having a grandfather of my own again."

Terri stepped away from him, unsure how to respond. She thought about his statement as she returned to the house and shut the door. For years, she'd enjoyed having Gramps all to herself and refused to spend time with her five cousins. Aunt Beth's two daughters and Aunt Maggie's daughter and two sons were all considerably younger, and Terri had no interest in sharing her precious Gramps-time with them or anyone else.

When she walked into the living room, Gramps was singing again. Age had not affected his robust baritone voice. She remembered him not only preaching but also leading music. Occasionally, he'd play the trumpet or xylophone during services. Her favorite memories were when he'd finish a sermon with a song. The ninety-year-old belted out, "My faith has found a resting place, not in device or creed. I trust the ever-living One, his wounds for me shall plead."

"I have to go." Terri gathered her belongings. The ease with which she conversed with Ethan unnerved her as much as the song Gramps sang.

Gramps readjusted the blanket covering his legs. "I wish you would stay."

She packed up a handful of files on a nearby table. "I have things to do."

"I don't understand why you drive an hour across town to visit with me and then only stay for a few minutes," he muttered almost to himself.

She refused to dignify his comment with an answer.

He waited until she picked up her car keys. "Are the Gaithers on?"

"I'll check." Terri reached for the remote, stood in front of the television, and quickly found the proper channel. "I'll see you tomorrow."

She blew Gramps a kiss and bolted toward the door. She had to get away. All this music put her nerves on the edge.

Terri arrived home later than usual on Saturday afternoon. Mr. Peterson had given her two tickets to see *Wicked* at the Belk Theater. She'd gone to the matinee by herself. Even considered giving the other ticket to Abigail but Terri saw no reason to interrupt her assistant's workday for the theater.

Once upon a time, Terri had been the one on stage. She'd never lost her love for the theater. The days when she had been an accomplished pianist and vocalist seemed a lifetime ago. She shook her head, refusing to think about that time when her heart soared with the music. A time when her heart had been one continuous song.

Terri wasn't sure she'd enjoy the show, especially in the beginning. But by the end, she felt sorry for Elphaba. She could commiserate with the witch most playgoers considered bad. Terri didn't see her that way. She wasn't bad, just misunderstood. Like Elphaba, Terri wasn't the popular girl but the one reviled and despised. People didn't understand why she shut herself away, and she chose long ago to stop explaining. *I'm not that girl.*

When she picked up the program and leafed through it again, her eyes widened in surprise. Mark Beaver's name was listed as one of the patrons. She'd not thought about him in years. *I wonder what he's doing now?* No, she refused to think about him. No need to go there. That was in the past. Best to leave it there.

Terri picked up the duster and strained to see the particles of dust covering her tables and wardrobe. The curtains should be open during the day allowing light to stream in, but sunlight gave her a headache. She reached over and turned on a low-watt lamp on her bedside table. Much better. Just enough light to see without bumping into the furniture, but not too much light.

Her clothes still lay on the floor where she'd left them. When was the housekeeper coming in? Terri wracked her brain and remembered she'd be there Tuesday morning. The woman had some serious straightening up to do. Terri ran the duster over the tables for a third time and then inspected the rag. Maybe the time had come to hire another housekeeper. She hated the thoughts of going through the process again but couldn't find a housekeeper who met all her needs. How many housekeepers had she hired and fired? Mrs. Anderson was the sixth or seventh she'd employed in the last three years.

While Terri worked around the house, she turned the television on and flipped through the channels until a decent movie appeared. She sat down and watched the last fifteen minutes of the mystery.

An hour later while organizing her closet, Terri heard Christmas carols blaring. Not again. Every channel she turned to played Christmas music. They were barely into December, and she already felt on edge. She turned to the local news. That should do it. She hurried to finish her project.

Ten minutes later, she climbed into bed, snuggled between the sheets, and tried to get comfortable. The news was still on, but she'd not paid it a lot of attention.

"We're outside the Belk Theater where *Wicked* is ..." the announcer began the segment. Her head snapped up, and she became engrossed in the news broadcast. If she'd not been there earlier in the day, she would have tuned it out, but now they had her attention. "We have Mark Beaver, who was instrumental in ..."

Terri stared at the screen as if seeing a ghost.

It didn't matter what was being said. She couldn't take her eyes off Mark.

He'd gotten better looking with age. Or was that even possible? Her eyes remained glued to the screen—or rather to Mark's face. Terri's heart pounded. Her mind moved back to the last time she saw him, or rather, refused to see him. So many what-ifs. She turned the TV off. Such a long time ago. She squeezed her eyes shut to blot him from her mind and readjusted the covers again, trying to change the direction of her thoughts.

Terri closed her eyes and pictured the numbers spiraling up on her bank account. She'd finished the initial plans for Mr. Peterson earlier in the week. He loved her design and told her they would break ground after the first of the year. Terri made a mental checklist of all the changes to make before seeking his final approval.

A thought flashed into her mind. She opened her eyes and stared into the darkened room. Where had that come from? She tried to divert her thoughts, but nothing worked. One name kept repeating itself. Strangely, it wasn't the one she thought might creep in. This one came as a total surprise. Terri couldn't shake the name or the feelings it produced.

She closed her eyes and tried to squeeze the name out, but it remained.

Over and over, she heard his name in her mind. *Ethan.*

CHAPTER 6

Terri was surveying the worksite when her phone rang.

"Can we meet?" Victoria Nelson asked when she answered.

"No." Terri hung up. She clenched her phone, regret building for giving the woman her cell number months earlier. But no regrets about her complaint. If possible, she'd have the woman's certification revoked. She'd made her decision and would stick by her actions.

Terri wasn't in the mood to deal with this bothersome woman. She needed something else to think about. She stared out at the construction site. *Why won't my mind stay here?*

Last night, she had arrived late at Gramps's. When she walked into the house, Gramps and Ethan were talking. At first, she thought nothing of their conversation. Originally, the growing friendship between the men had been touching, but now she felt threatened.

"Call me Gramps," the older man had told the younger.

Terri had stopped in the kitchen, her hands curled in anger. She didn't mean to eavesdrop but couldn't help it.

"Are you sure?"

She tiptoed to where she could see the men.

"Of course, son." Gramps placed a hand on his shoulder.

Noise from the construction site pulled Terri out of the memory. She jumped. With her nerves on edge, she decided to distance herself from Ethan. He seemed too young but was probably around her age. She realized when she looked in the mirror that forty-three was not so young anymore.

She turned back to her work. Lifting the camera to eye level, Terri snapped more pictures. Once again, Ethan came to mind.

"This *has* to stop." She'd thought about him way too much lately.

Then she remembered the rest of the conversation from the night before.

"Do you think Terri would go out with me if I were to ask?" Ethan asked Gramps.

Really? A date? She had slumped into a kitchen chair and held her breath.

"I wish she would." Gramps sounded wistful. "I think it's best if you wait a while. Continue to build a friendship with her." Gramps knew her all too well.

She did not like the feelings the budding friendship with Ethan evoked. He was a nice man and came to her mind *way* too much. Now he wanted to date her. She had to do something. But what?

"She's scared." Ethan's observation had grabbed her attention.

"Very." Gramps acknowledgment fueled her anger. How could he betray her this way? He knew what happened.

Concern flickered in Gramps's eyes when she appeared a moment later. He didn't say a word. And neither did she.

The conversation played throughout her mind for the remainder of the evening. Whenever Terri closed her eyes, she saw Ethan's face and the caring in his eyes. She wasn't sure how to label such an emotion. All she knew was this man had to stop plaguing her dreams—both the daytime and nighttime ones.

A scream snapped Terri from her trance. Metal crashed behind her. She spun around, running to discover what happened—the memories of the evening before momentarily forgotten in the moment of crisis.

That evening, she walked into Gramps's house ready to discuss some scaffolding which had fallen earlier on the jobsite. Thankfully, no one had been hurt, but she needed his advice to make sure it didn't happen again. As she entered through the kitchen, she looked through the glass partition between the two rooms to see the men deep in conversation.

Ethan sat on a short stool next to Gramps's recliner, his Bible open in his hands. "Last night, I was reading in Acts. Made me think. If Saul can have such an experience on the Damascus Road, then surely nonbelievers today can have such a conversion."

Gramps reached for his own Bible. "I agree. Nothing is impossible with God."

Ethan looked up to the older man. "How do you keep praying without losing faith?"

"Faith isn't always easy." Gramps paused. "Sometimes I wonder if God hears me."

"Does he?"

"Always," Gramps assured him. "We live in a society where seeing is believing." Gramps flexed his fingers as he often did when they grew cool. "But faith is believing what you can't see. All I know is God has shown Himself faithful too many times in the past for me to doubt Him."

"I wish I had your faith," Ethan admitted to the old preacher.

"Don't sell yourself short, son. You have a hunger for God and others, especially those who are hurting." Gramps patted the younger man on the shoulder. "You ask questions and seek the answers. A lot of men and women claim to be Christians but aren't willing to take the time to get to know God and His Word on a more personal basis."

"How's the patient?" Terri interrupted, walking into the room. She didn't want to hear anything else from either man about his faith and had to turn away from the intense compassion in both men's eyes.

"Good." Ethan rattled off Gramps's vitals. "Oh, I almost forgot. I promised I would bring you something." Ethan handed Gramps a tiny donut bag.

Gramps pulled out a chocolate-covered, crème-filled donut from the bag. "My favorite. Thank you." He wasted no time taking a huge bite into the delicacy and offered up a winning smile.

Fifteen minutes later, Terri checked his blood sugar, which had spiked twenty points. Not enough for a shot of insulin, but definitely something to monitor. She seethed with anger at Ethan for bringing the treat.

How dare he? What gall! First, he intrudes on our lives. Then he takes Gramps's time from me. Her mind raced as she counted off all the man's crimes.

After kissing Gramps goodbye, she headed toward her car.

Ethan was too friendly and expressed an interest in her. Now, he brought Gramps treats he didn't need. Worst of all, she couldn't get him off her mind. Terri made up her mind right then and there. Time to take action. Now. Before this man encroached into their lives any further. She dialed the

Carol OF THE ROOMS

number and waited for someone to answer as she put the car in gear. "I need to speak with your director. *Now!*"

She pulled out of Gramps's driveway, her plan in place. *Time for Ethan Brown to go.*

CHAPTER 7

Excitement welled in Terri as she pulled out from the Peterson jobsite. She enjoyed this project and could already envision her design on the property.

The last few weeks had proven difficult. Gramps had been livid when he discovered she was the reason Ethan had been fired. He'd never been this angry before. "I love you, but at this moment I'm ashamed of you," were his exact words upon learning of her actions.

She'd never known disappointment could cut so deep as Gramps continued.

"You've become a cold-hearted, selfish woman. What happened to the loving little girl I raised?" Gramps appeared as a broken man at that moment.

For just a second, she'd had a twinge of guilt. Then her hardened veneer returned. "She's gone," Terri snapped at her grandfather before storming out of the house.

She stayed away four days, the longest she'd ever gone without seeing him. Upon her return, she heard him praying for her. She wanted to run away again but forced on a brave face.

She sensed Gramps was still in communication with Ethan, but he never mentioned it to her. Then he sent her into another tailspin. "I've invited Maggie and Beth over for Christmas with their families." He held her gaze, determination in his eyes.

She stomped her foot like a child, determined to have her way. "I will not have it."

"Listen, little girl." She recognized this tone from her childhood. "They are my family, and I will spend the holidays with them if I so choose. I hope you will join us, but if not, it's your loss." For the first time in years, Gramps stood up to her and laid down the law.

She called both aunts and left messages. "If you're not gone by the time I arrive at three o'clock, I'll make sure you have no access to visit Gramps again." Terri wasn't sure how she'd pull that feat off, but she'd figure something out. Never one to make idle threats, she cringed at the thought of dealing with Gramps's irateness over the situation.

Terri pulled herself back to the present and reached into the visor for her sunglasses, one hand on the steering wheel. The sunlight blinded her.

At least Christmas will be over next week. She'd had enough of the festive holiday season and longed to concentrate on her projects in the works. The first check from Mr. Peterson had cleared the bank this week, and she couldn't think of a better Christmas present for herself.

She believed having Ethan fired would erase him from her mind. Sadly, this had not been the case. He continued to plague her thoughts. Everywhere she turned, she wondered where he was and what he was doing.

In the last day or two, her conscience had gotten the better of her. *How could you have had him fired? How is he going to get by financially? Being fired makes it so much more difficult to find a job.* All these accusations ran through her mind continually. No matter how much she tried to dismiss these thoughts, they continued to creep in.

Carol OF THE ROOMS

I refuse to dwell on it. What's done is done. I will not change my mind.

Terri glanced over to the side of the road. Did something move? It looked like pointed ears and a black nose. She shrugged and kept driving. Her imagination apparently decided to play tricks on her. Around the curve ahead, a black Labrador retriever ran in front of the car. Terri slammed on the brakes. The car spun out of control. Around and around she went. Trees waited straight ahead. She tried to prepare herself for impact.

I need help! Her mind raced. *Me? A self-sufficient woman.* She hadn't needed help from anyone in years.

Now there was no one who could or would help her.

Jesus loves me, this I know ...

Where did the sound come from? She'd not heard the familiar childhood song in years.

"God, help me!" she cried from the depth of her soul. A place she didn't know still existed.

Then everything went black.

CHAPTER 8

Terri opened her eyes, expecting to see trees around her, not the bright light that greeted her. All she could see was white.

Where am I?

This had to be a dream. Nowhere on earth was so white or bright.

Her mind couldn't comprehend what she saw. Everything shimmered as beams of light seeped in from every angle. No sky, no walls, no floor, no ... anything.

Below her were soft, fluffy objects like clouds. *Am I floating?*

Something or someone floated toward her. Terri squinted as the form neared and took shape. She could make out the blond hair and sea-green eyes she'd known so well.

"Marlee?" She blinked at the sight of her friend in a beautiful white gown. Her face glowed with an otherworldly glimmer.

"Am I dreaming?"

Her friend extended her arms in greeting. "No, Terri. Welcome."

"Am I dead?" There was no other explanation. Terri reached out and embraced her best friend and mentor.

Marlee stepped back and looked her over. "The situation's a little more complicated."

"I ... I don't understand."

"No, you wouldn't." *Looking good there, friend.* Marlee's thoughts invaded Terri's mind without a word spoken. *Your heart still needs a lot of work, though.*

How could she possibly hear Marlee's thoughts? *Where am I? Is this heaven? How is Marlee here?*

Marlee answered her unspoken questions. "This is like a holding place for souls with one foot in the mortal world and the other in the spirit one."

Terri cut to the chase. "So you're saying I have one foot in the grave? Am I dying? I'm not ready to die."

"Only God knows."

"So where is the big man?" Terri nonchalantly looked around for the supreme being her family had spent their lifetimes serving.

"Please don't be so blasé about all this. The Lord loves you." Marlee squared her shoulders. "That's no way to refer to the King of Kings and Lord of Lords."

"Yeah, I've heard." Terri sneered at her friend. The two women observed one another for a long moment. She could expect such a comment from Gramps, but never from Marlee. What happened to her?

"He—" Marlee reached for her.

Terri stepped back. "I need to get back. I've got projects to finish." She had so much to tell Marlee now that they were together again. "Do you remember Ray Peterson? We tried for so long to land his account. Well, I—"

Marlee laid a hand on her shoulder, gently interrupting. "Terri?"

Terri held the woman's gaze. "Yes?"

Carol OF THE ROOMS

"I tried to tell you before." Marlee stopped speaking until she had Terri's full attention. "You're living for all the wrong reasons."

"So you said. If there's not money, what is there?"

Marlee's eyes filled with sadness. "So much more."

"Like what?"

"Loving others. Caring for others. Living a life for others." Marlee counted each item on her fingers.

"All I hear is others, others, others." Terri placed her hands on her hips and stared at her friend. "What about *me*?"

"You've lived for *you* long enough." Marlee's voice held a hint of compassion. "Don't you remember? Jesus said He came not to be served, but to serve others."

Terri let out a frustrated sigh. "Yeah, I've heard it all before."

"I wish I could get through to you." Marlee closed her eyes. "God, please help her." Then she disappeared.

CHAPTER 9

Once again, Terri stood alone. "I've got to figure out a way back." She spun around. Everything remained very white. No signs, landscape, or directions. She'd never seen anything like this before.

"Who are you talking to?"

The voice made her jump. Who was it? Why couldn't she see anyone? "Myself." She turned in a complete circle.

"Where are you?"

"Here." The man came out of nowhere and appeared to be walking on a sea of glass. He wore a white robe, and his face glowed even brighter than Marlee's. He was the most beautiful creature Terri had ever seen, with perfectly chiseled features and blond hair that cascaded down his back. And those eyes. The clearest blue she'd ever seen.

"Who are you? Where am I? What am I doing here? And how do I get back home?" Terri couldn't take her eyes off him.

"I'm Gabriel."

"Like the angel?" Terri pinched herself. She didn't wake up.

"Yes." Suddenly, enormous white wings appeared.

"The one in the Bible?" Her eyes widened as she remembered where in the Bible he appeared. "The one who proclaimed the coming of Jesus?"

His eyes twinkled with amusement. "So, you've not forgotten?"

Terri heard a faint, muted sound she wasn't sure how to describe. She tried to block the annoying noise from her mind. "Forgotten what?"

"All you learned about God as a child." Gabriel's eyes continued to twinkle. She apparently amused him.

The sound grew louder and louder. Something vaguely familiar. "I guess not. At least not all of it." She let out a sigh, hating to admit the truth. "Gramps takes every opportunity to remind me."

"He loves you."

"He's the only one." Her heart sank. She had no one to blame but herself. She'd pushed everyone away. Not because she wanted to, but because she couldn't bear being hurt again. Was that music she heard? Her heart groaned.

The angel stepped closer to her. "Others love you, but you have to allow them close enough to—"

"Look, I've got to get back." Terri continued to search for an exit.

"Why?"

"To make money."

Gabriel held his arms out. "What will your money get you here?"

Terri stepped back. White light continued as the only scenery. She had no answer to the question, and the music blared now. Over the next few minutes, she made out the words. She recognized the song. Her nose crinkled. No one else seemed to be around. "Where is that music coming from?"

Gabriel's smile lit up his face.

"Why is it playing?"

"Because God loves music." Gabriel had the most beautiful, peaceful expression.

Terri couldn't understand how anyone could love music. "For what reason?" For her music carried too much pain with too many negative memories.

"Music is an expression of the soul." Gabriel hummed along.

Terri faintly made out the words: *Angels we have heard on high, sweetly singing o'er the plains.* "So ... how does God expect us to use music?"

Gabriel stopped humming. "In worship, plus as a form of self-expression."

And the mountains in reply ...

Terri looked around but saw no one else. "Who's singing?"

"The angels."

"Music is annoying. I mean it—"

"Nothing is wrong with music. God loves it, and at one time you loved it as well."

"I guess." She did not want to remember those days. "If there's nothing wrong with expressing oneself this way, then where are the dancers?" She sounded sarcastic but didn't care.

Suddenly, angelic dancers appeared and twirled around her. At least a dozen women, each with long, flowing hair, all dressed in white. As they twirled, they created an amazing array of colors, colors as vibrant as the elegant dancers who appeared to float on air.

Terri watched for a moment. "Okay, I get it." The music irritated her as much as how easily the dancers appeared.

Gabriel clapped his hands, and the dancers disappeared. "Dancing is one way of expressing yourself to music, but there are others."

"Such as ..."

"Art. Drama. Writing."

Terri blew out a long breath. "Okay. You made your point."

"Music is the soundtrack of our lives. The mood of the song can express our hearts and thoughts in various ways."

Terri's frustration almost got the better of her. "Why are you telling me this?"

When Gabriel raised an angelic eyebrow, Terri realized she'd overstepped her bounds. "Be ... cause," he drew the word out. "You're about to go on a journey."

"Where am I going?"

"Three spirits will visit you and take you on your voyage."

"Wait a minute." She took another step back to look at the angel. "What is this? *A Christmas Carol?* This must be a joke."

"If that's what it takes." Gabriel's clear blue eyes held a knowing look. "On your journey, you will not only see but also hear the soundtrack of your life."

"What soundtrack?"

Gabriel winked and disappeared.

ROOM I–THE PAST

CHAPTER 10

"I wish everyone would stop disappearing!" Terri bellowed.

Suddenly, she found herself moving through time and space, while her surroundings remained the same. Light shone through every crevice of the room. The brightness overwhelmed her. *How am I not blinded?*

A young girl approached. The child's light-auburn hair was enhanced by the whiteness of her robe. She carried a candle, which softened the room. The light gave the illusion the child floated on a cloud. Her amber eyes practically danced with glee, and she sang a song about sunshine and being happy Terri had learned as a child.

Terri groaned. *More music ...*

The spirit cast her a quizzical look. "What's your problem with music?"

Someone else reading my thoughts ... She groaned again. "That's not a carol."

The girl raised large amber eyes to hers. "Did Gabriel say you'd only hear carols?"

"No, I just assumed." Terri looked around. Why did she make such an assumption? "Maybe because 'Angels We Have Heard on High' played when Gabriel appeared."

"That is his theme song. He uses the song to announce his presence."

"Okay." Terri's curiosity piqued. "So is 'You Are My Sunshine' my theme song? That doesn't sound like me."

"At one time, it would have been."

"You're saying these songs won't all be carols?" Terri tried to understand this strange situation. *But why should I care? Music gets on my nerves.*

The girl stepped closer. "Do you know the definition of a carol?"

"No."

"A carol is defined as a song of joy." The spirit studied Terri. "I believe Gabriel mentioned the soundtrack of your life."

"Yes. So what does that mean?" *Do I really want to know?*

"Just that. The songs will express your heart at the moment in question."

"Okay." How could this be? "You Are My Sunshine" definitely did not express her heart at the moment. She wasn't sure what song would express those feelings. *Not sure I even want to know.*

"Time to go." The girl reached for Terri's hand. "Time for the truth."

CHAPTER 11

Clouds unfurled into scenes from Terri's life. She blinked. *Are we watching these scenes or being transmitted into them?* The entire scenario felt surreal. No use trying to analyze what was happening. She would never understand. She looked around but couldn't recognize her surroundings. "Where are we?"

The spirit held a finger to her mouth, evoking a familiar feeling.

What is it about her?

Terri turned back to the screen—or whatever it was—and watched the action unfold.

Terri saw her younger self standing by the Christmas tree in front of the bay window in her childhood home, only a few blocks from Gramps's. She remembered this room well. On the other side of the room stood a piano, the first one she had ever played.

Then she saw them. Her parents. Terri stepped closer, unable to get enough of them. It had been so long since—

I can't think of that now. Her eyes remained glued on her mother and father.

Daddy handed her five-year-old self a small package. "Open this one."

"Music books," she squealed after unwrapping the package. "Thank you." Jumping up from her seat on the floor, she flung her arms around Daddy's neck. Then the scene repeated with Mama.

"You've been asking. We think it's time you learn to play." Mama and Daddy both beamed with pride.

"Can I accompany you when you sing?" Her eyes widened in hope.

Daddy gave her a wink. "We'll see."

"I remember this Christmas," Terri said to the young girl beside her. Tears filled her eyes. "This was our last—" A sob escaped. She turned her attention back to the scene unfolding before her.

Mama waited until they finished opening the presents. "How about some pancakes?"

Young Terri clapped her hands. "With blueberries?"

"I don't see why not."

"We have exciting news," Daddy announced an hour later while the three gathered around the breakfast table.

She squirmed with excitement. "What is it?"

"We—" he pointed around the table. "The three of us are moving."

"Where are we going?" She took a bite of her pancakes.

"Mama and I have been praying and feel God wants us to serve Him on the mission field."

Young Terri took a sip of her milk. "What does that mean?"

"We will go where the mission board sends us and tell people about God's love."

"But aren't we doing that with Gramps?" Daddy worked with Gramps in his evangelistic ministry. She and Mama regularly attended services and helped Mimi anyway they could.

"We are, but God has different plans for us."

"Who will help Gramps?" She adored her grandfather and didn't want to leave him.

"I don't know, sweetheart. If he needs help, God will send someone."

"Where are we going?"

"We don't know yet," Daddy said.

Mama and Daddy exchanged a look. *Should we share our news? Should we wait? So many details we still don't have answers to.*

Terri felt weird hearing her parents' thoughts as she watched this scene from her childhood.

The scene shifted to later in the day. Terri and her parents were at Gramps's house.

Gramps closed his eyes and remained silent a long time before responding to her parents' announcement. "If God is calling you, then you have to follow."

"Let's play dress up," Aunt Maggie grabbed Terri's hand and pulled her from the room. Her aunt looked so young. Maybe around seventeen.

"We used to have fun dressing up in Mimi's old clothes. My grandmother loved vintage clothes. My aunts and I took great delight in trying them on." Terri turned to her guide and stared at the girl. *Why does she look so familiar?* The light on her candle flickered and lit her face. Terri gasped. *It can't be.*

Before she could speak, the scene changed again.

Daddy motioned to her from the pulpit. "Terri, will you join me?"

She jumped to her feet and rushed to join him.

"My young daughter has been singing this song around the house, and I'm so proud of her. I want her to sing it for you now." Terri gazed at him with pure admiration. "Proverbs 22:6 directs us to teach a child in the way they should go, and they will not depart from it." Daddy placed a hand on her shoulder. "What better lessons are there to teach our children than about the love of God?"

"This was his last sermon," Terri whispered to her guide. "At least, the last sermon I heard him preach." Sadness engulfed her. She watched and listened as the younger version of herself sang "Jesus Loves Me."

A sob escaped her as something in her heart broke.

Daddy smoothed out the back of Mama's hood on her coat. "Do you want to stay with her?"

"She has a cold." Mama turned to Daddy, who helped her slip into her winter coat. They stood in the hall outside Terri's room. "I thought about it, but I promised to lead the women's Bible study."

"We could take her with us and find a place for her to rest." Daddy tapped his chin as he mulled over the situation.

"The movement and open sea air isn't good for her." Mama had always been the practical one.

"I guess you have a point." Daddy scratched his temple, the way he did when in deep thought. "I'll call Mama and see if she'll keep her."

"Terri will love that. She loves to spend time with your parents and sisters."

"I'm afraid my sisters spoil her too much. Remember when Maggie and Beth took her shopping. They returned with three bags of clothes." He chuckled.

Carol OF THE ROOMS

"They love her. I'm grateful." Mama smiled at her husband.

Daddy kissed her. "I am too."

"I was thinking ... she'll be terribly disappointed about not going on the trip."

"It can't be helped," Daddy said.

"I know, but we can ease the blow."

Daddy looked confused. "How?"

"We'll tell her." Mama rested her hands over her abdomen.

Daddy lovingly reached out to caress her waist. "Let's wait until we've returned from the revival."

Terri gasped at what she saw. "I have a brother or sister?" She couldn't believe it. When younger, she'd always longed for a sibling. "I didn't know. I ... didn't know."

Her guide held out her hand. "Time to go."

"No, I don't want to go," Terri cried out. "I can't bear it."

Her parents had so much life in them. They were passionate about spreading the gospel and going to the mission field. And now they would be giving her a baby brother or sister.

"Why?" The cry escaped her lips from deep within. The pain so guttural she didn't know it was there. How long had she been carrying this pain? She turned away, unable to view what happened next.

CHAPTER 12

Terri covered her face with her hands. The events penetrated her mind's eye, preventing her from blocking it out. *Let it stop. Please, let it stop!*

She looked up and saw herself sitting on Gramps's knee.

"Ride the horsey." He laughed as she giggled with delight.

"Do it again," she begged when he stopped.

"One more time." He bounced her again as the doorbell rang.

"I'll get it," Mimi called from the kitchen where she prepared lunch. Terri had been with her grandparents for a week. She finally felt better after three days in bed. Mimi and her aunts catered to her lovingly.

"Is that them?" she called between gales of laughter. She loved time with her grandparents but couldn't wait to see her mother and father. They called every night to check on her. She missed them terribly. The night before, she sang a new song for them that Gramps had taught her: "He's Got the Whole World in His Hands." She smiled as Daddy joined in after the first verse.

"Clarence!" Mimi howled. Everyone ran to the door. It wasn't her parents.

Terri strained to see whom Gramps and Mimi were talking to. Beth and Maggie pulled her from the front door, back into the living room. They encircled her as a heaviness descended over the room.

"Enough!" Terri shrieked from her place in the scene. This moment was forever burned into her memory, and she didn't need to revisit it.

Screams emanated from her five-year-old self with the terrible news her parents had been killed in a boating accident on the way home.

Home. To her. If they hadn't been coming back for her, they would still be alive. *It's all my fault. They died because of me.*

Terri watched as Sophia, the family's twenty-year-old housekeeper, appeared and wrapped her arms around the inconsolable child.

"She helped me through that difficult time." Terri turned to her guide. "Sophia sang to me and stroked my hair until I fell asleep. She didn't leave my side for days."

The scene transformed again, and Terri stood at her parents' grave. She threw a rose into their joint plot before Sophia guided her away.

Sophia turned the young Terri toward her and kneeled to look in her eyes. "They'll always live with you in here." She pointed to Terri's heart. "They loved you very much. Never forget that." The child shook her head, unable to find words to speak. "You can always visit them in your heart, but you can also come here and pay your respects."

The spirit watched Terri as she observed herself as a child.

Terri shifted uncomfortably under the scrutiny. "Okay, so I've not been to their graves in years." Her defenses rose. She turned and glared at her guide.

Carol OF THE ROOMS

"Why not?"

"You should know why," Terri muttered. "After all, you're me."

CHAPTER 13

"Why are you doing this to me?" Terri's temples throbbed.

"Because you need to remember."

"What? Pain?"

This guide, this spirit, seemed to stare right through her. "If that's what it takes." Silence ensued for a few moments. "You also had good times."

Terri wanted to vomit at the song about sunshine and happiness when nothing but pain surrounded her. She folded her hands, pleading with the spirit. "Please stop that music." She gagged as nausea rose within her.

"The song proves you were once young, innocent, and happy."

Terri huffed. "That was a long time ago."

"Maybe, but somewhere deep inside is that youthful exuberance and innocence you've hidden."

"Things change. I grew up."

"Let's go to a happy time."

Terri wanted to fight these scenes with all she had. But no matter how hard she tried to block them, they penetrated her mind. She couldn't escape, no matter how much she longed to.

The scene changed again, and they were in church.

"God loves us so much He sent his only Son," Gramps preached at a revival. "He sent His Son to die on the cross. Most of you know I lost my only son and his wife three years ago. Their deaths were the worst pain I've ever felt." He glanced over at eight-year-old Terri swinging her legs in her seat. "I can't imagine how difficult it was for God to send His only Son. Knowing from the beginning His Son would die. To watch Jesus on the cross and the agony He endured." Gramps wiped tears from his eyes. "That's love. And why did He do this?" He glanced around the congregation. "Because He loves me, and He loves you. He sacrificed so we can spend eternity with Him."

Young Terri stood and answered the altar call. Gramps beamed as he led her in the sinner's prayer.

"I remember this. I asked Jesus to forgive my sins and come into my heart that evening," Terri said to her guide. She recalled the love and unconditional peace that overcame her hurting heart, along with the love and joy in her grandfather's eyes. "He baptized me in the river that spring."

"Sit still." Sophia laughed as Terri fidgeted and tried to get up. "I'm almost finished." The chestnut-skinned girl braided Terri's long locks down her back.

Young Terri wiggled in her seat. "This takes forever."

"It wouldn't take so long if you'd be still," Sophia reprimanded her.

Maggie skipped into the room. "What's going on?"

"I'm trying to get her to sit still," Sophia made a face as if she were angry.

Terri wanted to throw her arms around her friend as she watched the scene. She turned to her guide. "Everyone knew Sophia adored me. She hovered over me like a protective mama bear. I miss her."

Beth entered the bedroom and found a seat on the hope chest at the foot of the bed. "Let's go shopping."

Maggie turned to her sister. "For what?"

"My date." Beth gave them an ear-to-ear grin. She'd been pining after Ben for months, and he'd finally asked her out. Beth was beside herself with anticipation.

Mimi appeared in the doorway. "What are my girls up to?"

"We're going shopping." Maggie gave her mother a hopeful look.

Mimi clapped her hands together. "Let's make a day of it." She loved to shop.

"What do you have in mind?" Beth stretched out her long legs.

"I don't know." Mimi thought a moment. "Let's see, we'll shop and have some lunch."

"How about a mani-pedi?" Beth wiggled her fingers in front of her mother's face.

"That depends on how long it takes you to choose your outfit for tonight." Mimi lovingly cupped her daughter's cheek.

"Can Sophia join us?" Hope shone on young Terri's face.

Mimi nodded. "I don't see why not? There's nothing so pressing it can't wait."

"Thank you, ma'am." Appreciation rang from Sophia's voice.

"For what?" Mimi wrapped an arm around Sophia. "You're family."

Sophia wiped a tear from her eye, although she tried to hide it. No one thought of Sophia as the help. As far as the Neely family was concerned, Sophia was family. The way Sophia mothered Terri and joked with Maggie and Beth, she apparently felt the same way, although she never admitted it to them.

"That was a good day," Terri told the spirit. "That's my last memory of Mimi. She ..." Terri couldn't finish. The next morning, Mimi had a fatal heart attack. Once again, Terri lost someone very special to her.

CHAPTER 14

Terri clenched her fists. "Why are we here?" She'd not thought of this place in decades. How she hated these teenage years. They had not been nice to her, and she wanted to blot them out.

"You'll see."

Terri stared at the spirit. *Is this the only response I get?* She braced herself for what lay ahead.

"Hey, preacher girl," a student called as Terri walked into the lunchroom of their middle school.

"Just ignore him." Her best friend, Abby Mason, stood behind her in line.

"How's the *orphanage*?" Dinah Young taunted.

Terri struggled with the insults. Two years earlier, they'd been good friends. Dinah had been to Gramps's home many times over the years on play dates. Terri never understood what changed to cause Dinah to tease her.

They made their way through the line and found a table.

"Anyone sitting here?" an unfamiliar voice spoke behind her.

She looked up to find the most handsome boy she'd ever seen.

Abby patted an empty seat. "No, join us."

Terri opened her mouth, but nothing came out.

The young man introduced himself. "Mark Beaver."

Terri stood there beside her companion and memorized Mark's strong jawline, emerald eyes, and the small scar over his lip—among other features—knowing he could disappear at any moment. She gazed into those piercing eyes, feeling as if they were seeing through her. "He was always a looker."

"He became your closest friend."

"I know. I could always count on him." A smile played on her lips. When was the last time she smiled?

The continuous music in the background changed. This time to a popular song from *The Wizard of Oz.*

In a blink, it was the following year. Dinah and four other girls surrounded Terri outside the schoolyard one day. The names they called her brought tears to her eyes.

"Leave me alone," she yelled.

Dinah poked her. "What are you going to do about it, preacher girl?"

"I ... I ..." Terri sputtered. Good question. How could she defend herself?

Mark approached. "I'll do something about it."

One girl narrowed her eyes. "Are you her boyfriend or something?"

The stare from those emerald eyes cut through her. "Bother her again, and you'll answer to me."

Terri had never seen him angry before. Now he had a seething look.

"Let's get out of here." He took her arm and led her away from the group.

"Thank you." She struggled to keep up with his long legs.

"I think it's time I teach you to defend yourself." Over the next few months, he taught her karate moves.

Carol OF THE ROOMS

The beat sounded off on "Over the Rainbow." The word *lullaby* rose an octave before plummeting. The scene flashed forward a few months. Terri dissolved in tears while Mark wrapped an arm around her. She leaned into his chest. "Why are they so mean?" Being near him comforted her.

"I don't know." Mark pushed her auburn locks out of her eyes.

"They make it sound like I killed my parents." She wiped the tears that fell. "I wish I'd been with them." She'd never admitted her feelings aloud before.

Mark gently squeezed her. "I'm glad you weren't. I'd have missed out on getting to know you." She'd never felt so safe.

That evening, she shared the day's events with Sophia.

"You'd be crazy not to marry that boy when you get older." Her friend ran a brush through her hair.

"Who? Mark?" Terri's eyes widened in disbelief. "He's just a friend."

"That's what you say now. Wait until you're older." She caught Terri's gaze. "He'll be more. Mark my words." She held a knowing smile.

"Oh, Sophia." Terri sighed. She looked in the mirror at her twelve-year-old face covered with acne and her mouth filled with braces.

"Stand up to those bullies." Sophia reiterated this to her for over a year.

"How?"

"Outwit them."

Terri stared at the carpet, feeling the heat on her cheeks. "I don't know how."

"Then figure it out. Mark hasn't taught you those moves for nothing."

Terri watched the scene with fascination. Then she concentrated on the music filling the room. *Why is the song skipping a beat now and then?* she wondered as she was transported back to the school.

"I've never seen Aunt Maggie so happy," Terri told Mark and Abby one day at lunch after recapping the weekend's events.

"Love will do that to you." Abby took a sip of water.

"She was a beautiful bride."

"Yes, very lovely. So was your Aunt Beth." Mark smiled.

Her other aunt had married a few months earlier. Terri had been a bridesmaid in both weddings.

Abby held a dreamy look. "Do you think we'll have such fancy weddings?"

They all daydreamed about falling in love and their weddings one day in the future when they were older. Terri had been too busy helping her aunts with their wedding preparations for the past year to think about herself. "I don't know. I guess I've not thought about it." She led the way into their classroom and took her seat.

"Hey, Terri," Veronica, a friend of Dinah's, called from across the room. "Look under your desk." The girl's eyes were filled with malice.

Terri bent over. Her breath caught in her throat. Lying on the linoleum floor, a dead rat stared up at her. The room spun. She ran out of the room to the nearest bathroom.

Abby entered the lavatory behind Terri, where she stood at the bathroom sink wiping her mouth with a paper towel. "Terri?"

"Leave me alone." She didn't want to talk to anyone. Nothing stopped the bullying. She longed to disappear.

Terri stiffened as those old feelings returned. The music started to drag.

Carol OF THE ROOMS

She turned to her guide. "Stop the music. There's something wrong," Terri cried. "Why is the song slowing down? The sound is awful."

"Your spirit's slowly being crushed. The meanness of these girls took a toll on you. Instead of standing up and fighting for yourself, you shut down. The music is expressing joy being stolen from your soul."

CHAPTER 15

"My spirit didn't stay crushed forever!" Terri shouted.

"It didn't?" The spirit narrowed her eyes, her voice dubious.

"No, things were better in high school. At least ..."—she squared her shoulders— "for a while." She stood up for herself more, and the bullying subsided—but not without leaving scars on her soul.

Terri turned back to the scene in front of her and recognized the long stairs outside her high school. This was her senior year. She saw Mark standing around the corner from the auditorium with something hidden behind his back, but she couldn't make out what. His eyes lit up when she turned onto the other end of the sidewalk.

But her head was buried in a book. Anxious to arrive home so she could find out what happened next in the story, she wasn't paying attention and ran into someone. Her head popped up. "Excuse me."

"Not. A. Problem. Doll." The hottest boy in school had a long drawl.

She drooled. "You're Chip Snyder." She dropped the book and gasped.

Chip retrieved the items. "And so I am, Miss Terri Neely." He tipped his hat with a tooth-to-tooth grin.

He knew her name. They had a few classes together, but he'd never given her the time of day.

"Do you have a date for the senior prom?"

She blinked. He asked her to the prom. Her, of all people. She'd not even thought about the dance and didn't plan to go. Until this moment. "No."

"Then may I escort you?" He was so handsome in his Stetson hat and cowboy boots.

"I'd like that." She lowered her gaze to the concrete sidewalk so he wouldn't see the excitement in her eyes.

"We'll dance the night away," Chip said with a monotonous voice as he took her into his arms and waltzed her down the sidewalk.

They sashayed right past Mark, but Terri didn't see him—too enthralled with Chip.

Hurt filled Mark's eyes. He threw away a purple lilac. Her favorite flower. They'd been friends for so long he knew her likes.

The spirit startled her from her trance. "Do you know what the purple lilac means?"

"No, but I always thought they were pretty."

The spirit's eyes widened. "First love."

"Chip was definitely that." Terri smiled dreamily at the thought of him and couldn't remember the last time she had stars in her eyes about anything or anyone.

"I'm not talking about *Chip*." The spirit bit out the last word.

"Mark?" Terri frowned. "We were just friends."

"He waited there to ask you to the prom."

"I never knew." Would she have turned down Chip Snyder to go with Mark?

Carol OF THE ROOMS

The spirit stared right through her, which was very off-putting. "He didn't ask because he didn't want to interrupt your happiness."

"Well, that was short-lived." As the scene changed, she and Chip kissed on the beach. Terri shook her head at the reminder he wasn't all he seemed.

"Come on," he said, trying to coax her into giving herself to him.

"No." She held strong in her beliefs. "I can't."

"And why not?"

"I told you. I'm waiting until I'm married." She'd made a promise to God years ago.

"Where did you hear that, from your grandfather?" He mocked her.

She pushed him away. "What if I did?" She would not change her mind.

"That stuff is outdated," he taunted.

"Not for me." She stood and dusted the sand from her arms and legs. "I'm leaving." Chip didn't bother to follow her.

The scene transformed to several days later when Aunt Beth visited. Terri stared into the sweet innocence of the infant in her arms. "Did I do the right thing?"

"Absolutely." Aunt Beth handed Terri—who loved spending time with her aunts and their children—a bottle. Bethany was Beth's first child. Maggie also had a little one, a son named Keith.

While they talked, a girl knocked on the door. "Can we talk?"

Terri's mouth opened wide when the back door revealed her classmate standing there. Dinah hadn't been to the house in years. Not since they were in elementary school. She stepped aside for the girl to enter. "Sure."

"Outside?" Dinah's eyes pleaded for understanding.

Terri looked around, unsure. Dinah hadn't been as mean the last two or three years, but the memories from middle school lingered. Was she being lured into a trap?

"Okay." Terri hesitantly handed Bethany back to her mother before following the other girl outside. They made their way to the garden and sat on the slider swing Gramps installed for Mimi years ago.

Dinah turned toward her. "I know this is a surprise." Her eyes held a message, but Terri wasn't sure what.

"Yeah."

"I've done and said some mean things to you over the years."

Terri didn't respond. What was there to say?

"I'm sorry." Dinah surprised her as genuine remorse shone in the girl's eyes.

"Why did you do it?"

"I wish I had a good reason. I don't." Dinah swallowed before continuing. "I guess I was jealous."

"Jealous?" Terri's hand went to her chest. "Of what?"

"My parents were going through a rough patch." Dinah looked away. "For a while, I thought they might divorce."

"What did that have to do with me?" Terri didn't understand. She'd give anything to have another day with her parents.

"I saw the love your family had for you." Dinah kicked the ground. "I was jealous. I wished my parents loved me the way your grandparents loved you."

"That's why you teased me?" This made no sense. "At least you had parents. I barely knew mine."

"I know and I'm sorry." Sincerity filled Dinah's hazel eyes.

Terri thought about her confession. "I want to forgive you, but I think it'll take time."

Carol OF THE ROOMS

"I understand, but I've got something to tell you."

Terri felt like a deer caught in headlights. "What?" Her heart pounded in anticipation.

"I didn't come here to hurt you." Dinah fidgeted in her seat. "But you need to know."

"Know what?"

Dinah sighed. "Chip is cheating on you."

Terri's mouth gaped open. "With whom?" Her voice broke.

"Abby Mason."

Before Terri could react, the spirit whisked her away to another place.

Sophia beamed as she surveyed the wedding dresses surrounding them. "You're looking more like yourself," she said to Terri.

"I feel more like myself." The last few weeks had been difficult. Terri cried, screamed, and cried some more. Chip betrayed her, along with her best friend.

Mark had held her and allowed her to cry until she had no tears left. He listened to her rant and rave in one breath and lovingly reminisce about the good times in the next.

"You're a good friend."

He only looked away.

What would she do without Mark?

Sophia brought her back from her woolgathering. "What do you think of this one?" She held up the next dress.

Terri shook her head. "Not really your style." It didn't seem possible they were here to pick out a wedding dress. At thirty-two, Sophia had finally found the man she wanted to spend her life with.

"Tell me about your trip." Sophia held up another dress.

Terri motioned for Sophia to keep looking. She shared her upcoming plans with Gramps. He would conduct revivals throughout Europe for six weeks, and Terri would accompany him. It excited her to head overseas and take in all the sights she'd heard about. While she talked at a fever pitch, Sophia held up one bridal gown after another. With each shake of the head, the wedding dresses went into one of two piles—*don't even think about it* or *try the dress on*.

"I can't believe you're getting married." Terri was happy for her friend.

After three hours of trying on dresses, Sophia finally found the perfect one. "Goodness, child, you won't even know I'm gone. You'll be in college."

Only two weeks to pack for school upon their return from Europe. Terri pointed to a veil. "I may be in college, but I wouldn't miss your wedding for anything."

"What about Mark?" Sophia raised a questioning eyebrow.

"What about him?" She didn't understand why Sophia kept bringing the subject back to her best friend.

"Will you miss him?"

"Of course, but I'll see him when I come home."

A knowing look filled Sophia's eyes.

Terri turned to the spirit. "What am I missing?"

CHAPTER 16

"Why won't you answer me?" Terri was becoming frustrated with this smaller version of herself.

The spirit's eyes filled with sadness. "The answer is right in front of you. You refuse to see it."

"What am I supposed to see?" She challenged the memory of her childhood.

The spirit pointed to another scene. "Look."

College. Terri loved college. She met the theater crowd and became involved in many productions. Her favorites were the musicals. She had roles in *The Phantom of the Opera*, *Jesus Christ Superstar*, *The Sound of Music*, *My Fair Lady*, and *Oklahoma*. She even appeared in a handful of dramas and comedies. For the first time in a long time, she felt alive.

The music of her life changed. A song about dancing all night played. This song didn't drag the way the previous one had. Quite the opposite. It became lively.

"You're living again," the spirit answered the unasked question.

Terri smiled. These were good times.

The scene merged into another. Terri sat outside on the theater steps as a man approached.

"I'm glad it's finally cooling down," a deep, male voice said.

"Same here." She smiled at the man as a large leaf blew across his head. Classes had not ended yet, and the walkway remained quiet.

He took a step closer. "Would you like some company?"

"Sure." She scooted over. Once he joined her on the steps, she introduced herself. "I'm Terri. Terri Neely."

He nodded. "I'm James Stewart."

Terri shook the offered hand. "Like the movie star?" She easily recognized the name, but this man was much broader and tanner than the Hollywood actor.

"Don't laugh. Mom thought it would be funny to name me after him."

"He must have been her favorite star."

James's beautiful teal eyes paired well with the copper hair peeking out from a ball cap. "No. Her favorite is Cary Grant. She saw all his movies." He grinned, making his eyes sparkle.

Terri had never seen such white teeth before. "The movies of which one?" She was enjoying his company.

"Both." They laughed at the joke. "Haven't I seen you around?"

"Maybe. I enjoy the theater." Again, they giggled at the irony of the situation. She turned to meet his eyes. "I hate to admit it, but you don't look like Jimmy Stewart."

"I know, which is why I don't use Jimmy. I'm James." His voice lowered. "I'm not sure whether the name is a curse or a blessing." Then he grinned broadly.

Terri grinned back. He was considerably shorter than the star, but she wondered in what other ways he might be different. Maybe it would be fun to find out.

Carol OF THE ROOMS

The scene shifted to a visit at Gramps's house. Terri often went home for the weekend and holidays.

Sophia grinned. "How is James?"

"Great." Terri grinned and held out her left hand. "Look." The diamond in her engagement ring sparkled in the sunlight streaming through the window.

"Wow, look at that." Sophia gave a low whistle. "How long have you been dating now?"

"Two years." Terri's voice held a wistfulness to it. "Hard to believe it's been that long."

Sophia's chocolate eyes twinkled. "Yes, things are certainly changing."

Terri cast her friend a quizzical look. "Am I missing something?"

Sophia clapped her hands in delight. "I'm having a baby."

"Oh, Sophia! That's wonderful." Terri set aside the embroidery in her hands and jumped up to give her friend a warm hug. "I'm happy for you. You'll make a wonderful mother."

"I hope so." Sophia studied her friend. "I have a favor to ask."

"Sure, name it."

"Will you be my child's godmother?"

"Of course. I'm honored." She danced a jig before hugging Sophia again.

"We were so happy," Terri mused thoughtfully from where she watched. Before she could say another word, the scene changed again.

"I'm getting married," Terri triumphantly announced to Mark later that night.

Mark froze. "What?" A look of hurt and betrayal filled his eyes.

"He. Was. In. Love. With. Me. How could I have never noticed?" Terri's legs buckled beneath her. She sank, but into what she didn't know. Then, as if by an unseen hand, she rose. A stool formed from a nearby cloud for her to sit on.

Understanding dawned. "How could I have been so blind?"

CHAPTER 17

Still reeling from the scene with Mark, Terri watched herself rush into the hospital waiting room. "How is she?" she asked Sophia's husband.

"I don't know." Terrance paced the floor. "They asked me to step out." Worry lines creased around his chestnut eyes.

"What's wrong?"

"She's in a lot of pain. Something isn't right." Concern filled his voice.

The wait seemed an eternity, but in reality, only lasted a few minutes before the doctors allowed them back into Sophia's room. Terri accompanied Terrance. Her friend's paleness shocked her. Her aunts had discussed how challenging childbirth could be, but Terri never realized it could be this difficult. She ran a hand over her friend's arm. "How are you?"

"I've been better." Sophia gave her a weak smile. "I can't wait to meet this little one." She patted her baby bump.

"That makes two of us." Why was it taking so long?

Terrance stepped out to speak with the doctor.

"Did I tell you the name we decided on?" Sophia asked.

"No, I don't think so." Terri would have remembered.

"Emma Terri." Sophia grinned before another contraction took her breath away.

Terri inhaled sharply. "Oh, Sophia." Her eyes watered.

The doctor returned with Terrance. "We need to perform an emergency C-section. The baby is breech, and we can't turn her around."

Sophia's eyes widened. "Is she going to be okay?"

"We will do everything in our power to make sure she is." The doctor wasted no time in issuing orders. Pandemonium ensued in the following moments.

Terri called James and asked him to come. She needed his support and for him to hold her.

"I can't. I have two papers due." He sounded distracted. "Besides, they are your friends, not mine."

She hung up, tears stinging her eyes.

In retrospect, she had ignored this waving red flag. *Danger. Danger. Danger.*

She walked back to the waiting room. As she turned the corner, Mark sat in a chair, obviously watching for her. What a welcomed sight. A sob escaped. "What are you doing here?"

Mark stood. "To be here for you. What's going on?"

"I didn't know you were here." She took the seat next to him and wiped tears from her eyes as she related her conversation with James and gave him Sophia's progress. He wrapped an arm around her and held her tight. She allowed herself to be consoled. "I'm worried about Sophia and the baby." She rested her head on his shoulder. Mark's presence comforted her. It always did.

Minutes later, Terrance appeared, his face drawn, worry lines creased his forehead. "She's here." He attempted to smile, but his eyes filled with uneasiness.

"What's wrong?" Terri walked over and placed a hand on his arm.

"Emma is fine. They are checking her over now. It's Sophia."

Terri's heart dropped. Sophia would be fine. She had to be.

"She's lost a lot of blood," Terrance explained. "They're giving her a blood transfusion."

Her head spun. This couldn't be happening. The sterile setting swam before her eyes. The doctor came out about thirty minutes later and explained Sophia's chances were fifty-fifty. Terri begged to wake up from this horrible nightmare.

After being led to the nursery a few minutes later, her heart filled with a love she never knew possible. "You're beautiful," she cooed to the infant. "Your mama will be so proud of you."

Terrance appeared shortly after Terri returned from the nursery. "She's ... gone."

"*No!*" Terri collapsed.

Terri couldn't believe what she saw from her viewpoint in the clouds. She turned to the spirit. "I never knew Mark caught me." He held her as sobs wracked her body from the depth of her soul.

The music around them dragged, to the point of stopping before resuming at a much slower pace.

CHAPTER 18

Terri continued to watch as the four months following Sophia's death passed in a whirlwind of activity. She kept herself so busy she didn't have time to think about the loss of her best friend.

Terrance called several times. Terri never returned his calls. All the love she had for baby Emma turned to hate. If it hadn't been for her, Sophia would still be alive.

The clouds switched to another scene. Terri and James lovingly stared into one another's eyes.

"I thought we were so happy," Terri whispered to the spirit. Her voice was full of emotion. "Was our relationship all an act?"

Suddenly, she twirled with delight and shouted from her hotel window. "Tomorrow, I'll be Mrs. James Stewart." This was the night before their wedding. Both their families had booked hotel rooms for the wedding festivities.

Joy filled her face, but this time James refused to make eye contact and acted as if something were amiss. His jaw twitched, and his eyes didn't hold the look of love she remembered. What had changed from the previous scene?

The clouds transitioned again to the church where they were to be married.

Glancing around the crowded chapel, she saw so many friends and family members. This was the day she'd dreamed about since they'd met. As she scanned the sea of faces, Terri paused on Mark. His eyes were filled with so much pain he looked as if his heart had been ripped from his chest.

Terri covered her face. "Please stop it. I can't bear it," she begged the spirit. The cry came from the depths of her pain.

The spirit remained kind but firm. "You need to see this."

"But why? Wasn't it enough to live through this nightmare once? Why do I have to relive it?"

"You'll see."

Terri uncovered her face and turned back toward the scene in front of her. She stood at the back of the church, waiting for the doors to open so she could walk down the aisle. She'd labored over all the decorations, including the violet and pink lilacs covering the altar.

The doors opened, and she began her slow descent down the aisle. Gramps stood at the front, waiting for her. He was the only person she'd wanted to officiate at her wedding ceremony. But where was James?

She continued to glance around. James wasn't there. Smiling faces turned to looks of sympathy. Murmurs and whispers began as she drew closer to the altar, but she couldn't make out the words.

Her aunts quietly disappeared behind the choir loft. When they returned, they shook their heads. Aunt Maggie whispered in her ear, "I'm sorry. James has disappeared." Her aunt wrapped an arm around her shoulders.

Carol OF THE ROOMS

Terri stood at the altar craning her neck while her mind spun in a million directions. *Where could he be? Why isn't he here? Was he in an accident? Has he been hurt?* Why wasn't Terri's intended waiting for her? She replayed the last few days in her mind. They'd been together at the rehearsal and the dinner after. James said nothing about doubts, although he seemed distant and distracted. She'd convinced herself his behavior was only nerves. That's when she realized she'd been kidding herself. Heat moved up her cheeks. As she wondered how he could humiliate her this way, the background music slowed and softened.

Terri watched herself run down the aisle and out the church doors. She rushed to her car and drove away.

Mark ran after her but couldn't catch up. He chased her for more than a block before giving up. He bent over, placing his hands on his thighs, panting.

Terri frowned at the spirit. "Why was he outside the church?"

"Let's look." The spirit replayed the scene. As Terri walked down the aisle past his seat, Mark stood and walked out. "He couldn't stomach watching you marry another man."

That's when Terri noticed no music played. "Why did the music stop?" She looked around expecting to find an answer.

"This was the defining moment in your life."

Why did this spirit always talk in such riddles? "What do you mean?"

"All the other heartaches got you down, but you continued to recover. This time you refused to bounce back."

"What?" Terri shook her head. "I bounced back. Didn't I? To business."

"This was the moment you gave up and refused to open your heart again."

My heart hardened. "But I'm still alive." Terri pinched her arm. "Well, sort of—"

"You've been existing, but your heart died years ago. You dedicated your life to money, power, and success. What do those things get you here?" She motioned to the light that emanated from every corner. "You can take only one thing with you," the spirit whispered, the way one does with a secret. "Love."

The silence became deafening.

CHAPTER 19

Then a new song began, very different from the previous ones. The notes were coarse. Dissonant. Harsh. Terri cringed. "What is that?"

"What does it sound like?"

Terri strained to listen. She finally recognized the melody. "Is that the overture to *The Phantom of the Opera*?" She never thought something like this would be on the soundtrack *of her life*. At least that's how Gabriel described this music. "Aren't they supposed to be happy and upbeat songs?"

"That's the hatred and anger in your heart you're hearing."

The piercing minor tones emphasized the revelation. Terri shuddered.

The scene shifted until she saw herself hiding at the lakeside cabin Gramps owned, sequestered after James humiliated her. Terri ignored the knock on the door until it grew more and more persistent. She finally opened the door. "What do you want?" she spat.

Mark stood before her, his face chiseled with worry. His clothes were crumpled, as if he'd not slept in the three days she'd been at the cabin. He tried to push the door open. "I'm worried about you."

She leaned against the door, blocking his attempt. "I'm fine."

Concern and confusion flashed in his eyes. "You don't look fine."

"Leave me alone." She slammed the door in his face. Didn't he understand? She didn't want to see him or anyone else. Much too embarrassing. She'd be happy to see no one—ever again.

Scenes flashed before her in quick succession, revealing Mark sitting outside her door until well after nightfall. When he left, he gave one last glance toward the cabin, defeat written across his face.

That is the appearance of true love. The voice was one she'd not heard in years. She recognized the voice, though. God whispered to her heart.

The spirit pointed to Mark. "He's offering you an olive branch."

"I was so hurt I didn't see it," Terri said in her defense.

"All you had to do was accept it."

"But I didn't." For the first time, Terri felt a pang of regret at her choices. She'd spent two weeks at the cabin shutting down all her feelings.

"You were never the same after you returned."

"I guess not." Terri's mind raced through her choices and decisions, but this time, she mixed in regret. "The week after my return, I met Marlee."

"And money became your primary focus."

CHAPTER 20

"Our time is ending," the spirit said. "But there is one more thing."

Terri squeezed her eyes shut. What could it be?

"You need to see something."

The scene switched to a barroom. Mark raised his fist to James. "How could you hurt her like that?"

"Oh, she'll get over it," James sneered. He mockingly raised his beer in a toast.

"I'm not so sure." Mark decked the smirking man. Without a backward glance, he strode from the bar, leaving James sprawled spread-eagle on the floor.

Terri gasped. "I didn't know." She surprised herself when she clapped. Mark had always been her hero, and she'd longed to hurt James for years after the shambles of their wedding.

"Mark loved you for a long time."

Sorrow filled Terri's heart. "Why am I only realizing this now?"

As the scene shifted, they found Mark in Gramps's living room sitting at the foot of Gramps's recliner, his head bent in despair. "She's not the same person. I don't know how to reach her any longer."

Gramps's voice was filled with sadness. "I know."

Tears fell down Mark's cheeks. "I keep praying, but she's angrier than ever."

"Don't give up." Gramps tapped the Bible on his lap. "So many people love her and are praying."

"I won't stop praying, but I can't wait forever." Mark's shoulders slumped forward.

Gramps laid a hand on top of the man's head. "I don't expect you to, son."

"I love her so much." Mark's voice broke as tears continued to fall. "I always will."

Gramps's own tears streamed now. "I know. Sometimes we have to leave those we love in God's hands."

"That's easier said than done."

"You've got to live your life, son. You've loved her since you kids were in middle school. For reasons none of us understand, a romantic relationship never worked out for the two of you."

Mark swiped the back of his hand across his cheek. "I've prayed and sought God's advice, but there's been one roadblock after another."

"I wish I had answers, but I don't."

The two men bowed their heads and prayed for Terri.

Terri shook her head. "I never knew," she said to the spirit. For the first time, she felt shame over her actions.

"You were too self-absorbed by this time."

Terri knew the spirit was right. Only one thing had mattered to her over the last two decades. Making money.

A new scene found Terri flipping through her mail, surprised to find a letter from Mark. She'd not seen him in over two years since that day at the cabin. He had tried many times to contact her, but she always ignored his calls and refused to see him the few times he came by to visit Gramps. She wasn't sure why she wouldn't see him. Other than he'd seen her deepest pain. She couldn't allow herself to be vulnerable to anyone, ever again. This included her best friend.

Running her fingers over his name on the envelope, she wondered what he had to say. Hesitantly, she broke the seal and withdrew the contents. She dropped it like it was on fire. This wasn't a letter but a wedding invitation.

Tears of sorrow wracked her body. As she threw the invitation into the fireplace, she sank onto the floor and collapsed into a ball of grief.

"That's the last time you cried," the spirit said sadly.

And the last time she'd been brokenhearted. "I didn't realize I cared so much. I didn't know how to love him." Shame rose within her.

The music changed again. A new song filled the air. For a fleeting moment, she remembered singing it when she starred in *Jesus Christ Superstar*.

"I never knew how true those lyrics would become. How different would life have been if I'd made different choices? What if I'd given Mark a chance?"

The spirit studied her.

The questions replayed until the young spirit disappeared.

Then everything turned bright white as light emanated all around her.

ROOM 2–THE PRESENT

CHAPTER 21

A moment later, the next spirit appeared, wearing a hunter-green robe flowing from top to bottom with full sleeves that fell down her arms and covered her hands.

"You look like me." Terri walked around and inspected the entity. "But you're not me." Something in her eyes and face were different. She looked … happy. Content.

The spirit readjusted the wreath of holly adorning her head. "I'm the you who *could* have been."

Why do these spirits always talk in riddles. "Please explain."

"You'll see. But first let's look at your current life." She held out a hand.

"Why would I want to see my current life? I know how I live."

The spirit held Terri's gaze. *Do you?* The unspoken question reverberated through Terri's mind and body.

Gramps's living room materialized, and Terri found herself immersed in the scene instead of watching it as she had in the past. With a wave of her hands, she tried to get her aunts' attention, but they did not acknowledge her.

Maggie's and Beth's children and grandchildren gathered. Terri hardly recognized them since she'd refused to see her cousins for years, and most of her cousins' children she'd never met.

"It's two o'clock. Terri will be here within the hour." Sadness filled Gramps's voice as the grandfather clock chimed the hour.

"I wish we could spend the holidays together." Beth looked wistful. "All of us."

"Me too. Terri hasn't been the same since—" Maggie shrugged.

Terri bristled as she listened. Everyone seemed to know how much she changed after James left her standing at the altar. She lost her heart that day. Her greed for money and prestige now took precedence in her life.

"He may have shared the name, but he definitely wasn't Jimmy Stewart." Beth scrunched her nose.

"No, Mark was the leading man in her life." Maggie glanced at a picture of a much younger Terri in a silver frame Gramps kept on his mantle. "She had so much life and spark back then."

"Sadly, everyone saw his love for her, except her," Gramps said wistfully as he gazed at the photo.

Beth looked around the group. "Do you remember when she was ten?"

"She would play the piano for us." Maggie sighed. "She was so talented."

Gramps glanced at the piano in the corner of the living room. "I don't think she's played in years."

"She had such a love and talent for music. Terri could play *and* sing," Beth said.

Maggie agreed. "I forgot she starred in all those plays and musicals."

"Yeah, she was good. Even had the starring roles in *Calamity Jane* and *The Sound of Music*." Beth sounded like a proud mama.

Carol OF THE ROOMS

"James ruined that as well." Gramps wrinkled his eyebrows. "Since then, she seems to despise music."

"I miss those days." Maggie shifted the child on her lap. "She came to life on the stage."

Beth shifted in her seat. "Is there *anything* she enjoys now?"

Gramps scratched the side of his head. His daughters waited while he thought.

"Checkmate," Keith called from across the room where he played a game of chess.

Maggie turned to her son. "One more game, then put it away."

"She used to play with us when we were young," Bethany added from across the chess table, her daughter on her lap.

"She loved you all." Beth ran a hand through her granddaughter's hair. Everyone gave her a dubious look. None of Terri's cousins seemed to remember her as anything other than the angry woman she'd become.

"I think she enjoys her photography, but I'm not sure if she realizes how much." Gramps ran a hand over his nose.

Bethany smiled adoringly at her grandfather. "And spending time with Gramps."

"Does she?" Gramps tapped his fingers on the arm of the recliner. *She acts as if she cares, but does she really? She'll drive from one side of Charlotte to the other daily. If she really cares, why does she only stay for ten minutes most days and seem preoccupied even then?*

Terri gasped at hearing her grandfather's thoughts. "I'm busy."

"Are you?" The spirit cast her a stern look.

Gramps sighed. *I'm lucky if we have a good hour-long visit twice a week. I'd rather Terri visit once or twice a week for an hour or two than to drive so far for such a brief stay. But she's refused to listen to my wishes.*

Hearing her grandfather's thoughts made Terri very uncomfortable.

Anne, Maggie's youngest child, piped up. "I can think of something she enjoys."

"What?" Maggie asked.

"Money."

The room fell silent.

The chimes in the living room tolled the half hour. Their time together was quickly running out.

When the scene changed, Terri stood in front of a dilapidated building. Nothing looked familiar. "Why are we here?"

The spirit said in an upbeat voice. "You'll see."

Terri ground her teeth at the jovial manner. The spirit took her hand and marched her inside.

"That's mine." A boy pulled the blanket from a little girl who couldn't be more than six years old. Her clothes were threadbare, but then again, so were all the children's.

May Patterson turned to face the child. "Alexander, why can't you and Mia share a blanket?"

"Why should I?" The towheaded boy with a tear-stained birthmark on his left cheek looked defiant.

"That's the woman from the orphanage." Terri recalled her visit a few weeks earlier. "She begged for a handout." The children shivered. "Why doesn't she give each child a blanket?"

"They don't have enough for everyone. They have to share." The spirit nodded toward the children huddled together for warmth.

"Then they should turn the heat on."

"There's no money for heat."

Terri's back arched. "That's ridiculous."

"Is it?" The spirit watched her. "They can *work* for what they need, right?"

Terri took a step backward. *I resent having my words come back to haunt me.* She turned to the spirit with a desperate plea. "Is there no one to help?"

"Like who?"

"I don't know." Terri shook her head as Mia climbed into bed with the other girls. The children huddled close.

"Aren't there enough beds?"

The spirit shook her head.

Mrs. Patterson had mentioned needing renovations because there was no room. Could this be what she meant? "What about toys to play with?"

"If there's not enough money for blankets and heat, how would there be money for toys?"

With no blankets and no heat, how could she even think about toys? "You've got a point." Terri soaked in the pathetic sight around her. "I never knew how difficult these children had it." Something foreign stirred in her chest.

The spirit turned to face her. "You were lucky."

"Lucky how?"

"This could have been you."

Terri froze. She was right. If Gramps and Mimi hadn't taken her in, Terri would have ended up in an orphanage. Aunt Beth and Aunt Maggie were only teenagers at the time of her parents' death and would not have been able to care for her.

The spirit seemed to wait for a response.

"At least as they grow older, they will forget these hardships and make a ton of friends." She could hardly put into words what she felt for these children. Terri needed to learn to be honest with herself before admitting she cared for another.

"Are you sure about that?"

"Everyone knows people don't forget the elderly. I mean, well ... there are always stories about elder abuse and people taking advantage of them." *I'm grasping at straws.*

"Just like you hear stories of child abuse." The spirit had a condescending tone.

Before Terri could comment, a new scene appeared. They stood in another building, some type of institutional structure. The concrete walls screamed at her, and the linoleum floor made her feet ache. She stared out the window at the leafless trees and wilted flowers in the courtyard.

The spirit pulled on her arm, and Terri turned around. Men and women sat in groups at round tables.

"My son said he can't come for Christmas," one man said between spoonful of soup.

"I'm sorry, Joe." The other man patted his outstretched hand on the table. "At least we'll be together."

"I guess, but your wife is here. So you're not all alone."

"No, I'm not alone. But my sweetheart doesn't know me most of the time, which makes me feel very lonely."

"Didn't your preacher come yesterday?" Joe took a sip of coffee.

"He did. Only stayed about fifteen minutes. Sometimes I don't think anyone cares."

"I know what you mean. My son said I always tell the same stories, but, Bill, they are what I remember."

"We've seen some tough times." Bill clucked his tongue at the memories.

"Brother, don't you know it." The conversation turned to their service in the war.

Carol OF THE ROOMS

Terri assumed they meant World War II. She turned and walked closer to a table with two women, one probably in her nineties. Her face furrowed in pain, and her hands shook violently every few moments.

"How are you today?" A worker, possibly in her mid-thirties, stopped at their table. She wore a name badge, but Terri couldn't read it from so far away. She seemed very familiar with the residents. *Looks like she works here.*

The older woman couldn't speak, but her eyes lit up with recognition. The younger woman caressed the older woman's cheek with her hand. "Hi, Lila Belle." The greeting came out in a singsong voice. Was this a routine with these ladies?

"She loves you." The second resident, probably in her late twenties, sat across the table. She was much younger than all the other people in the room.

Terri wondered what caused this young woman to come to live in such a place.

"I love everyone here." The worker's smile seemed genuine. She turned to the youngest resident. "How are you today, Kathy?"

"Okay, but I didn't sleep good last night." Kathy lifted her juice glass from her tray. With one hand she attempted to remove the top and almost dropped the cup.

"I'm sorry to hear that." The worker caught the glass before it fell. With even hands, she removed the top, inserted a straw, and safely replaced the glass. For the next five minutes, she provided a sympathetic ear as Kathy shared her troubles. "I've got to go, but I'll see you later this afternoon."

Kathy nodded before the woman walked away.

Terri crossed her arms. "One person to care for how many?"

The spirit held out her hands. "Many feel abandoned and all alone."

Terri turned back to the table with Joe and Bill.

"Sometimes I think my son dropped me off here so he wouldn't have to worry about me any longer." Joe laid down his silverware.

"How long since his last visit?" Bill asked.

Joe wiped his mouth with his napkin. "Six months."

"Where does he live?"

"He's only a twenty-minute drive away."

"I'm sorry, my friend." Bill patted Joe's shoulder then bowed his head. "Lord, show us how we still matter. We feel abandoned and forgotten some days. We want to make a difference for you, even at this stage of life."

"Why are you showing me this?" Terri balled her fists. "I don't know these people. I can't do anything for them," she hissed. "I didn't put them here."

This is precisely why I don't want Gramps in a facility.

CHAPTER 22

The scene and music changed. A disconnected and disjointed melody plucked along.

Ethan hung up the phone. "Terri, what have you done?" His voice held a note of despair, which echoed in the empty room.

Only silence greeted him.

"I would have loved her. I know she's hurting but didn't realize how selfish she is." He walked over to his spider plants then slid onto the floor. "Please, Lord, be with Terri. Help her. Restore her damaged heart. She needs You, Father."

Terri stepped closer to Ethan. "He has no idea I'm here, does he? I've never heard someone pray with such fervency."

The spirit shot her a knowing look.

"Okay, that was a lie. I've seen Gramps and Daddy pray fervently many times." She turned back to Ethan.

"God, You brought me to this, and You'll bring me through it. I pray for Your provision. You know my needs. I pray especially for Terri. She needs You, Lord. Her heart is ugly with selfishness."

Terri swallowed the lump forming in her throat.

"I don't know the circumstances in her life, but You do, Father. I ask You—no, I beg of You—give her a Damascus Road experience. Help her come to know You. Tear down those walls in her heart. Melt the ice running through her veins. Pursue her until she can no longer run. Help her to not only come to know and love You but also to know what true, unselfish love is. Show her the love that can only come from a relationship with You ..." Ethan continued to pray out loud with intense passion.

Terri's hands shook.

The music changed to a darker melody. *This must be a minor key, given its harshness.* "That music is awful. Turn it off." Terri covered her ears and glared at the spirit.

"You should be familiar with it." The spirit seemed unaffected by her mood.

"What?" Terri lowered her hands. "Why all the riddles? I don't know this piece."

"You may not know it as Domenico Scarlatti's 'Fugue in G minor,' but you know it for the discord and disjointed moments that have made up your life."

"How dare you!" Terri snapped. The screeching music, sounding like nails on a chalkboard, irritated her.

"How dare I what? Speak the truth?" The spirit's voice remained steady.

Terri pointed her finger at Ethan. "Ethan is only one person. He'll be okay. I'm sure he'll find another job." *I must admit he's a wonderful nurse.*

"Maybe, but he's not the only person you've treated in such a manner."

"What do you mean?" Terri angrily tapped her foot while the music shrieked.

"I'll show you."

"I don't want to see." Terri turned away and closed her eyes.

Carol OF THE ROOMS

The spirit touched her shoulder. "You don't have a choice."

Even with her eyes closed, Terri could see Ethan on the floor. The music grew louder and more disjointed. "Fine!" she spit out. "But first stop that awful music."

"As you wish." The spirit held out her hand, and the music changed. The new song sounded even more disconnected and disjointed than the first.

"That's worse." Terri covered her ears again to block out the noise, but it grew louder. She felt the melody—or lack of it—rise from within her. *The music is within me.* She slapped her hand to her forehead.

"You can't change the melody revealing the color of your soul."

"What do you mean, the color of my soul?" Terri knew her voice sounded harsh.

"Every soul has its own color. It experiences what it feels in the moment."

"Can the soul only be one color?"

The spirit grinned. "Of course not. As our moods and perceptions change, so does our soul. The music only manifests the color expressing our soul."

Terri shook her head. More riddles. "I don't get it. The color?"

"The happiness and joy or the pain and hurt. Others may show doubts and jadedness or depression and anxiety."

"So what's my color?"

The spirit refused to meet her eyes.

"Tell me."

The spirit remained silent.

"Is it that bad? If it's too late to change the color of my soul, then why show me all this?"

"I didn't say it was too late to change. It's never too late to change." The spirit looked into her soul. "I said you can't change the melody exposing the color of the soul."

"So what is this piece?" Terri wasn't sure she wanted to hear the answer.

"'The Cat and the Mouse' by Aaron Copland."

The scene morphed until they stood in a living room. Terri didn't recognize the stylish room but saw a woman sprawled across the couch with her head buried in her arms while she sobbed. Terri instantly recognized the woman.

Victoria Nelson.

Victoria's words seemed to bounce off the walls. "I *hate* you, Terri Neely!"

"Who am I?" A young man counted an imaginary stack of bills as they arrived in a new location.

Another young man laughed. "You must be Emma's Aunt Ri."

"Come on. She can't be that bad."

Terri stared at the people in front of her. *At least someone defended me. But who are these people? And what happened to Victoria?* "What are we doing here?" she asked the spirit.

Emma entered the living room carrying a tray with a Christmas wreath pinwheel appetizer that appeared to be stuffed with sausage.

Terri had never been to Emma's house, which was now decked out with an abundance of Christmas trees, snowman decorations, and a train set in the corner. *This is so Emma.* Her goddaughter's friends sat around a living room described as fashionably chic.

Why am I being shown all these people I don't want to see?

Carol OF THE ROOMS

Emma had Sophia's eyes and apparently her heart for others. *How is it possible Sophia has been gone twenty-five years?*

Terri turned her attention back to the conversation.

"Aunt Ri's not *that* bad." Emma's lips tightened.

Derrick stood for his turn at Pictionary. "Emma has blinders on when it comes to her Aunt Ri."

"She's a wounded animal." Emma provided a sad smile to the group.

"There's no reason to treat people the way she does."

Emma brushed away a stray tear. "She wasn't always this way."

Terri felt uncomfortable at this display of emotion. *Why did the girl always see the best? Probably because Terrance taught her well.*

"Then what happened?" Derrick asked.

"Several things."

"Will she be here for Christmas?"

"I hope so. I invited her." Emma's eyes sparkled with hope.

"Emma invites her every year, but she never comes." Derrick drew his card. "I, for one, am glad. I don't want her negative energy in our home."

Emma gasped in surprise. "Derrick!"

"I'm sorry, baby. I know you love her, but I can't seem to like her."

Emma's eyes brimmed with tears. "But it's Christmas."

"Yes, and that's the time to celebrate the birth of our Lord and Savior, Jesus Christ. If she can't remember the true meaning of Christmas, then I don't want her here."

"She reminds me of Ebenezer Scrooge in *A Christmas Carol*." One of the young men imitated the miser.

"Maybe we need to pray for three spirits to visit her," someone else said.

Everyone except Emma laughed. She formed a prayer circle. "Let's pray for her heart to get right with God."

Terri whirled around in indignation. "I've seen enough." Each note in the music became more separated and disconnected.

The spirit chuckled. "Not yet. One more stop."

"Where are we going now?" Terri glanced around the tiniest basement apartment she'd ever seen. The living area appeared no larger than Terri's walk-in closet, with an attached miniature kitchen and a small room in the back. Apparently, a bedroom.

A woman sat at a kitchen table with a stack of envelopes in her hand. "I don't know what to do."

Terri frowned. "That's Abigail. What's happening? Why are we here?"

"All in good time. Pay attention."

"How am I ever going to pay all these bills?" Abigail asked an older woman. From the resemblance, Terri assumed this to be Abigail's mother.

The woman laid a reassuring hand on Abigail's arm. "Somehow we'll manage."

"I'm working as many hours as I can manage, but even that's not enough."

"Ask for a raise."

Abigail let out a harsh laugh. "I'd be fired."

Terri held back a laugh. *She sure would be.*

"You could find another job."

"I've thought of that."

Carol OF THE ROOMS

Terri's eyes burned with fury. Abigail was the best assistant she'd ever had. Would she really consider leaving?

Abigail reached for her mother's hand. "I don't know what I'd do without you and Dad to help."

"We wish we could do more." Her mother looked at the ledger of debts.

"If only I could pay for his surgery." Abigail's voice was barely above a whisper.

Terri turned to the spirit. "Who is she talking about?"

"Shh ..."

"I can't lose him." Abigail wiped a tear from her eyes. "I can't!"

The sliding glass door opened, and an older man entered carrying a young boy on his shoulders. "We'd better duck," the man called to his passenger.

"We're back," a young boy said as the man bent low enough to get them both through the door.

Abigail put on a brave smile. "Did you have a good time?" She quickly wiped tears from her eyes.

"We did. Grandpa and I chose a real evergreen tree."

The man bounced the child on his shoulder. "To be delivered this afternoon."

"Then we can all decorate." The boy squealed with delight.

"What's wrong with him?" Terri wrinkled her forehead in consternation, but the spirit didn't answer.

The boy's grandfather tenderly lifted him from his shoulders and carried him to a nearby chair.

"Why isn't he walking?" Terri stepped over to the chair. He had to be at least five or six years old. Old enough to be walking, that was for sure.

The spirit pointed to his legs. "He can't."

"How could I not have known about this?" Terri couldn't believe how blind she was to her own assistant.

The spirit raised a questioning eyebrow. "Do you even know his name?"

Terri shook her head. "No, I don't."

"It's Timmy."

"Will he die?"

"Only God knows." The spirit lifted her eyes toward the heavens.

"Why show me this if it can't be changed?" Terri demanded.

"Life is what we make of it."

"But it can't be changed. None of this makes sense. If things could change, then people would transform themselves."

"Says who?" The spirit held her gaze.

"If life could be changed, I would do it in a moment. I tried to alter the past." Terri's voice grew higher and louder. "I tried everything I could think of." She let out a guttural cry. "Nothing worked."

"The past can't be changed."

Terri threw her arms out to the side. "That's what I just said."

"But the future can."

"How? I need to know. If it can be changed, then how do I change it?"

"By the choices you make today."

Terri thought for a few moments. "Such as? Help me understand."

"You have to decide for yourself." The spirit turned back to the scene at Abigail's.

Timmy sang, and the family joined in. "God rest ye merry, gentlemen."

The spirit sang along. Her eyes sparkled with merriment, and her entire face came alive with a word Terri couldn't conjure. Then it hit her. *That's what's different. She's happy. Alive in her heart.*

"What did you mean when you said you're the me who could have been?"

The spirit ignored her and continued to sing.

Terri bellowed at her, "I need answers—and I need them now!"

CHAPTER 23

"You could have had a different life," the spirit said.

Terri rubbed her temples. "What do you mean?"

"The choices you've made have led you to this point."

"Okay. I'm trying to follow."

"Different choices led to a different outcome."

Terri's temples continued to throb. "Such as?"

The cloud ahead morphed into a scene. "Let's look."

They returned to the cabin.

"What are we doing here? Why are we rehashing this moment—again?"

"Watch."

Terri saw herself alone in the cabin, curled in a ball on the floor beside the fireplace. She had cried until she couldn't weep any more. A knock sounded on the door. At first she ignored it, but the sound became more insistent. She finally pulled herself up from the floor.

"Mark!" Her mouth fell open when she cracked open the door. "What are you doing here?"

"I'm worried about you." Mark pushed the door open halfway. They stared at one another. "May I come in?"

Terri considered the request. "I don't think—"

"I'm a good listener." Mark stuck his foot out to prevent the door from shutting.

Finally, she shook her head and opened the door wider. "Okay. Come on in."

Terri looked at the spirit. "The music has changed." She looked around for signs of the popular love song that had replaced the dissonant sounds. The song had been a hit when she was younger and talked about longing for the touch of another. This was much better than the awful music which had been playing.

"You changed your future." The spirit nudged her with an elbow. "Watch."

Terri and Mark sat on the couch and talked for hours. At one point, their gazes met and held. He wrapped an arm around her.

Terri laid her head on his shoulder. "James hurt me so much."

Pulling her closer, Mark held her as she sobbed.

Scenes sped by of them talking. At first, she was sad, but then she smiled and finally laughed. They took walks through the woods. She saw many scenes of them on the lake in Gramps's boat fishing or swimming. They laughed as they took turns dunking one another in the lake.

Terri's heart warmed at the scene before her. *When was the last time I laughed?*

Then the scenes slowed until they landed on the couple, standing on the dirt trail at the mouth of the lake.

Mark placed his hands on her shoulders. "I will miss this."

Terri gazed adoringly into his eyes. "Me too."

"I don't want to go back."

"Me neither." They looked at one another for a long time before either spoke again. "I'm glad you came." She kicked the ground, suddenly feeling shy.

"That makes two of us." He tilted her chin up, his breath on her face. Both afraid to move. Neither wanting this moment to end.

"There's something I've wanted to do for years, but—" He stepped back, dropped his hand, and then stepped closer again.

Terri's heart skipped a couple beats.

Mark wrapped an arm around her waist and pulled her to him. With his left hand, he pushed a stray strand of hair behind her ear before caressing her cheek. "I have to know." His words were barely a whisper as he tipped her chin up. Lowering his head, his mouth brushed against hers. First softly and then with an intensity she didn't know he possessed.

Terri wrapped her arms around his neck. Eagerly, she returned his kisses.

"I love you," Mark whispered in her ear.

"I love you too," Terri whispered back.

Terri glanced at the spirit. She could hardly believe what she was hearing. *I really do love him. All this time I thought I loved James. Those feelings are nothing compared to what I feel for Mark.*

"I thought I'd lost you," Mark whispered between kisses. "When James—"

"James who?" Their laughter broke their kisses.

Terri turned toward her companion in surprise. "Why can't I seem to accept the truth that he loved me?"

The spirit nodded. "Why do you think he came that day?"

"What would have happened to us? What might have been?"

"I'm not sure you want to know."

"No, I do want—have—to know." *More than I ever thought possible.*

The love song continued to play. Terri thought of the scene in the movie *Ghost* where Molly longs for Sam to come back to her. Sam could do nothing but wait for her to join him one day.

The scene changed, and Terri stood in the back of the church.

"I've already seen this. How could you—" Fresh betrayal washed over her. "This is a sick joke, taking me back to the worst moment of my life."

The spirit touched her arm, her eyes dancing with happiness.

The doors opened, and Terri began her descent down the aisle. This time, her groom stood at the altar. It wasn't James. It was—

She gasped. "I married Mark?" Her heart pounded. *I could have had a happy life. How could I not have known how Mark felt? Would it have made a difference? Would I have done things differently?*

As she reached the altar and took his hand, Mark beamed when he saw her.

"We are gathered here ..." Gramps began the wedding ceremony.

"Are we happy? I have to know. Is Mark my true love or rebound guy?"

Again the scene changed, and they were at Gramps's home. Judging by the decorations, Terri saw it was the holidays.

"Who wants to hear the Christmas story?" Gramps called from his recliner. Christmas tree lights bounced off the wall above his head. Maggie, Beth, and their families gathered round.

"I do," a voice called from the kitchen, echoed by several other childish voices. The patter of little feet ran from the kitchen to the living room.

"It's my turn." A little girl tried to climb onto Gramps's lap. The child was the spitting image of her.

"No, it's my turn." A little boy joined the girl on Gramps's lap. They squirmed for space with the old man.

"Now, children." Terri appeared in the doorway with a baby on her hip.

"You can both sit in Gramps's lap." Mark appeared behind his wife. He took a bite of the candy cane-shaped sugar cookie in his hand before wrapping an arm around Terri.

"But you have to be still," Gramps reminded them.

Terri's heart jumped with excitement. "We had children. I never even dreamed about that possibility." A tear rolled down her cheek, followed by another, and then another. For the first time in over a decade, Terri Neely cried.

Then something inside her broke. "I lost out on so much. All because of my anger. I could have had all that?" The truth slowly sank in. "I've been so foolish." *Too bad this parallel life can't be real. Things would have been so different. I would have been so different.* Her heart plummeted. *There's no hope now.* Terri let out a long sigh as she wiped tears from her eyes. "No one cares for me now."

The spirit wrapped an arm around her. "More people care than you realize."

CHAPTER 24

"What do you mean? How could anyone care for me? A lonely miser. How could they? After the way I've treated everyone. I've been mean and selfish to people." A weight seemed to lift with the admonition of truth.

The spirit nodded in agreement. "Yes, you have."

"How could anyone care when I've treated them the way I have?" The faces of her family and friends hovered before her.

"I want to show you something." The spirit spoke so low Terri strained to hear. *Is this some type of conspiracy?*

The music changed from the love song to something different.

"Is that a hymn? That's the last type of song I expected, but I'm not sure why. Aren't all hymns about God?" *Though your sins be as scarlet, they shall be as white as snow.* "I've not heard that in years."

Terri's body seemed to be floating again. That was the only way she could explain their movements. "Where are we going?"

They immediately stopped.

"Right here," the spirit answered. A variety of scenes filled the whiteness of the room. The images before her appeared so luminous.

"How are they doing this? Am I watching multiple images on various TV screens? It doesn't look like TV screens though. It looks more like each scene playing through a cloud or some type of heavenly window. Nothing makes sense here." Then she heard a voice.

My ways are higher than your ways.

Terri swallowed the huge lump in her throat. The scenes floated all around her, making it difficult to concentrate.

First, Gramps sat in his chair, hands folded over his Bible.

Ethan knelt on the floor by his couch.

Her aunts held hands at the kitchen table with their heads bowed.

Emma knelt beside her bed, a soft glow of candlelight flooding the room.

Abigail sat outside on a porch rocker, staring out over the garden.

"What are they doing?" Each person seemed lost in their own thoughts, as if they were ... *No. Ridiculous.*

The spirit nodded to Victoria on a swing. "Isn't it obvious?"

"They appear to be praying." *Victoria?* Terri had never seen her as a committed Christian. *Even as angry as Victoria is, she's praying for me?* An emotion Terri couldn't describe washed over her.

"They are."

"Why are they all praying? For what?"

"For you."

Terri's mouth fell open. "Me?" Her voice faltered.

The spirit nodded.

"Why?"

"For you to come to know God's love."

"Why should I? After He's let me down?" *Why did the words feel so hollow?*

"Because God loves you."

"Then why did He allow such tragedy to happen?" Terri scratched her head.

That deep voice spoke again. *You're making this more difficult than it should be. There are always things you will never understand.*

Terri looked around in surprise. *Who was that?* No one else seemed to be around. *Did the sounds come from above?* "What good do all these prayers do when—"

"More good than you think." The spirit sighed. "You are hardheaded."

The music changed to a praise hymn Terri remembered singing in revivals with Gramps. The song shared a message about people needing the Lord and wondering when they would realize their need.

"Why are these songs playing? And how are these songs the soundtrack of my life?"

"These people love you." The spirit lifted her hand and motioned to those before her.

Terri hung her head. "I don't deserve it." Sorrow filled her heart.

"You're right. You don't."

Terri didn't appreciate the honesty. The two stared at one another before Terri turned away. *I want to escape the scenes, but images are everywhere.* To the right. The left. Up above and down below. Everywhere.

"Your family sees the heart. These songs show not only their hearts but yours."

"I don't get it." Terri moaned. She ran a hand through her shoulder-length hair, tired of not understanding. "Why can't I grasp it?"

"You don't want to understand. This is the moment of truth. This is what you need most."

"What?" Terri snapped, fresh irritation rising from within.

"God's love."

"How will that help me?" Terri muttered to herself.

"More than you'll ever know."

Terri stiffened. She had to gain the upper hand.

Why do you fight Me?

"God? Is that You?" Terri trembled. "Why won't You leave me alone?"

Do you really want Me to leave you alone? I pursue My children until they are ready to return home. Do you want to keep living the way you have been living? To reject Me for all time? Are you ready for those consequences?

Terri turned to the spirit. "Show me Mark."

"I don't think it's a good idea."

A deep longing washed over her. "Why not? I have to see Mark."

The spirit refused to meet her eyes. "I just don't."

"I want to see how he's doing." Terri's nostrils flared.

"All in good time."

Terri remembered him on the news program. "He looked so handsome on TV. What would I have done if I'd run into him at Belk Theater?" She let out a long breath. "Probably rebuffed or ignored him." *Why, Terri? Why do you act this way?*

Terri looked around for the spirit, who waited, pain contorting her face. "Show me Mark." she hissed.

Sadness filled the spirit's voice. "I can't."

"Is he still married?"

No answer.

"Is he happy?"

The spirit shook her head. "I can't tell you anything about him."

Terri clenched her jaw. "I'm not used to being denied." She shook her fist at the spirit. "I want to see Mark, *now!*" she growled.

Show her where he is at this moment. The voice reverberated around them.

The spirit reached into the scene of Emma kneeling by her bed and took the candle from the nearby nightstand. "This is all I can show you."

The light flickered and enveloped them. Mark appeared, worry and sadness carved across his face.

Terri frowned. *Something's wrong?*

He knelt on a bench in church. "Father, it's been years since I've seen her, but Terri has been heavy on my heart tonight. Wherever she is, whatever is going on in her life, be with her. I pray You will watch over and protect her. Above all, bring her back into your fold. You promise when one sheep leaves the fold, You will go after that sheep. She's left your fold, and I beseech You to go after her and pursue her with a vengeance. Help her know You and Your love. Restore her to the young girl I befriended and later loved. I know somewhere underneath all those layers of anger and hardness, the innocent young girl still exists."

Terri's heart twisted. Mark had kept his promise to Gramps. Even after all these years, he still prayed for her.

The spirit disappeared, and the room grew still. Mark and the other scenes dissipated. Light again encompassed her.

Terri wiped away the tear that rolled down her cheek.

I miss Mark.

ROOM 3-THE FUTURE

CHAPTER 25

"I don't need this. Get me out of here!" Terri screamed. *Why doesn't anyone listen to me?*

The room dimmed until only a shadow remained.

A dark figure, covered from head to foot in black, approached. A black hood hid the spirit's face and flowed onto the floor.

Terri took a step back. "Are you the me of the future?"

The spirit nodded, but Terri couldn't see her eyes.

"Do you speak?"

The spirit shook her head.

"I'm not that dark and menacing. And I don't like to be reminded of death."

The spirit raised a bony hand, which was nothing more than a skeleton.

"What—"

They moved through time and space until they stood in Terri's bedroom. The curtains were drawn. Darkness enveloped the room. She lay on her bed, the sheet and comforter drawn all the way to her chin.

Music played again. *Nearer, my God, to Thee, nearer to Thee ...*

"We sang this in Gramps's crusades." Terri stepped closer to the bed. "That can't be me. I'm nothing more than skin and bones. I look like …" *I can't go there.* She looked around. "Who are these other people?" Then she recognized her lawyer and housekeeper.

Tom, her lawyer, had a look of disgust. "Has anyone been to visit?"

Mrs. Anderson, her housekeeper, shook her head. "No one."

"She had so much going for her." Tom looked away.

Mrs. Anderson sighed. "If only she'd not been so obsessed with money."

"The takeover did her in." Tom inhaled sharply. "After the way she's treated people, it's hard to feel sorry for her. But I do."

Terri scowled. "What takeover is he talking about?"

The spirit pointed at the scene.

"I'm not saying it's right, but I don't blame Abigail," Tom said.

Terri took a step toward Tom. "What did Abigail do?"

Mrs. Anderson shook her head. "Do you know what happened to him? Such a sweet boy."

Tom stood with his hands behind him. "That poor boy developed cardiovascular issues as his limbs grew stiffer, and he was unable to move."

Mrs. Anderson made a tsk, tsk sound. "I never knew cerebral palsy could lead to death."

Tom continued to stare down. "His atrophied limbs led to his untimely demise." He choked up. "It broke my heart, it was so sad. Abigail did all she could but couldn't afford the surgeries that poor child needed."

"Poor Abigail. I'm afraid Timmy's death was too much for her." Mrs. Anderson gaze fell to the figure on the bed. "Abigail learned her lesson too well."

Carol OF THE ROOMS

Terri looked up at the entity. "Who did she learn from?"

Tom huffed. "I've never met a more selfish, uncaring person."

"I guess you would know." Mrs. Anderson turned to straighten the room.

"As her lawyer, I've witnessed her demise firsthand." He raked a hand through his hair. "I hoped there would be a different outcome."

"All those years of praying. My heart breaks. I wonder why God didn't hear our prayers." Mrs. Anderson looked up at the ceiling.

"God heard. He even sent chances. Sadly, Terri refused to take them."

"Have you talked with her family?"

Tom looked surprised. "What family?"

"Doesn't she have cousins?"

"Yes, but they said, and I quote, 'We tried for years, and she wouldn't give us the time of day. After the way she treated Gramps in the end, why should we care? Terri never cared for anyone else.'"

"What happened to Gramps? I'd never do anything to hurt Gramps."

The music slowed.

As the days sped by, no visitors arrived. Only Mrs. Anderson stopped by daily with a bowl of soup.

Terri watched herself try to sit up and eat. After a few bites, she lay back exhausted and fell asleep.

The next scene made Terri seethe. "That's my office building. What happened to Jacobson and Neely?" The sign read Walker Architectural and Interior Design.

Before she could ask more questions, she saw a man hiding in the alleyway on the side of the road leading to the firm. A young woman, maybe in her early twenties, pulled into the lot and parked her Chevrolet.

"What's going on? Why am I seeing this?"

The spirit pointed.

The young woman opened her car door, stepped out, and walked toward the office building.

The man stepped from his hiding place. "Hand me your money."

The woman's eyes widened in fear. "Please, no."

Terri recognized the tear-stained birthmark on the boy's cheek and gasped. "It's Alexander, the boy from the orphanage. How did he get here?"

Alexander grabbed the woman's purse.

"Please," the woman begged, pulling on the strap. Fear flashed across her face. A gun accidentally fired.

Alexander released a string of obscenities and fled. Police sirens wailed in the background.

"Where is he going?"

The spirit pointed, and the music changed. A funeral march played. The music dragged ... so ... so ... slowly.

The boy raced down the street. He looked over his shoulder, but apparently knew where he was headed. Alexander ran down one street after another on a mission. Finally, he stopped in front of the city cemetery and paused long enough to gasp a breath or two before continuing. He ran through the cemetery to the very back where he stopped.

"What is he—"

He knelt in front of an unmarked grave. "I'm sorry, Mia." Tears rolled down his cheeks.

"The little girl?" Terri's hand went to her mouth. "What happened?"

"I was a rotten brother. I should have been nicer to you," he spoke to the gravestone.

"Why are Alexander and Mia so important? Why show me this?"

The spirit continued to point.

Abigail stood in the distance. "What is Abigail doing here in the cemetery?"

A moment later, Terri stood beside her assistant. "Timmy?" How could this be? She blinked trying to take it in. Even though she had just learned of Timmy's death, seeing his name on the tombstone startled her. "Timmy couldn't have died, could he have? Why did he have to die?"

"Nothing's the same now," Abigail said to the grave. "I would give up everything to have you back. My marriage to Wallace is over. You never met him, but maybe that's a good thing." She pulled her wool coat tighter around her. "I thought money could buy anything and everything I wanted, but it can't." Abigail bent down and wiped the debris from her son's tombstone. "I didn't realize how happy I was when you were alive."

"Why didn't Timmy get his surgery?" Terri wanted to spit fire at someone. "Tell me it didn't have to be this way."

The spirit said nothing.

Terri let out a frustrated cry and stomped her foot. "Couldn't something have been done to save him?"

The spirit pointed to Abigail standing before her son's grave.

"If I'd had the money when you were alive that I have now ..." Abigail shrugged. "I could have paid for your surgery." She straightened the flower arrangement. "You know, it's true what they say. Money can't buy happiness." Then she let out a low, sarcastic laugh. "I learned from the best, but I'm afraid I learned too well." She glanced around as if she felt someone watching her. "The mighty Terri Neely. She may have had a heart of stone, but she sure had a savvy business sense." She paused and looked around again. "Well, at least savvy money sense."

Terri bristled. "What's wrong with that? Why is being financially savvy so bad? Better than living in poverty."

When the spirit pointed to Abigail, the music stopped.

"My old boss died this morning." Abigail shook her head. "I take that back. They said she'd been dead for two days. No one checked on her." She wrapped her arms around herself as a shudder moved through her body. "Mrs. Anderson brought food but had been out sick herself. Tom checked on her weekly. If she'd not paid them, no one would have known she died. I wonder how long it would have been before anyone might have found her."

"I—" Terri gasped for breath. "Show me."

They shifted a few rows over to her tombstone.

Terri struggled to breathe.

"Thank you." Tom shook the undertaker's hand. He turned toward the newly shoveled ground. "I feel sorry for you," he spoke to the dirt-covered coffin once the undertaker left. "You lived for yourself and died for yourself. No one even bothered to come to your funeral." A rush of wind blew past. Tom reached up to brush the hair from his eyes. "You were so worried about money and died practically penniless. What irony." He let out a sad guffaw, then bent over and swiped some dirt from his shined shoe. "I will do what you refused to do. With the eight hundred dollars left to your estate, I'll do good with that money. I don't know how, but there's plenty of people in need. I'll find someone to help." His shoulders went back with determination.

Police sirens blared. A moment later, three squad cars entered the cemetery.

Carol OF THE ROOMS

Tom watched as the police cornered a young man at a grave in the back. "Is this the person I should help?" He looked toward heaven then walked toward the commotion.

Utter darkness enveloped Terri. She couldn't make out any shapes or designs. A tear ran down her cheek. She'd never felt genuine fear before. Until now.

CHAPTER 26

Am I dead? Darkness continued to engulf her. Terri lifted her hands in front of her face and couldn't see them.

"Oh, God, please help me!"

"Do you mean that?" a voice spoke through the blackness.

Terri looked around but saw nothing. From far away, a small flicker appeared.

"Yes."

The light moved closer.

"I don't want to die all alone."

"Who does?" The voice made a valid point as the glow neared.

"I don't." The light grew closer. "Who are you? Can I change my future? I'd give anything to alter this dismal outcome."

"Our decisions always have consequences which affect our future." The light gleamed now and revealed the angel Gabriel.

"So I saw." Terri's body shook. *No wonder Ebenezer Scrooge changed his ways.*

"Did you learn anything?" Gabriel's golden hair flowed around his shoulders, creating a halo over his white robe.

"I not only saw the consequences for my actions but also what might have happened had I chosen better." That's what troubled her. Things could have been so different. *Why did I have to wait until someone else showed me? I should have realized this myself.*

Gabriel nodded. "So, what did you learn?"

"Some consequences are for the better and others for the worse. Until James, I kept my heart open and willing. After being hurt, I closed myself off to everything and everyone except making money."

He nodded. "That's good."

"Is it too late to change?"

"We can't change the past, but we can always change the future."

"That's what the spirits said."

"They were right. You can start today making changes for the better."

"How do I know how to make the right decisions? I've made so many bad choices. Can I change my thought process? My life?"

"Yes, by seeking God's will."

"Does He really love me? How can God love me as much as He promised? Doesn't He know all I've done?"

"Let me show you how much." Gabriel waved a hand, and they were transported to a hill. Nothing looked familiar. Soldiers carrying swords walked around in gladiator tunics and feathered hats.

"Are those real Romans? Where am I?"

"What do you see?"

She stared at the unfamiliar costumes. "A lot of people. Most of them seem to be—" She stared ahead. It couldn't be. This had to be some crazy dream.

They were on a hillside. There were three men, each ...

Carol OF THE ROOMS

Gabriel watched her, not the scene. Neither said a word as she struggled to process the vision before her.

The crowd jeered and called out vile things. Three men hung on a cross. The man on the right asked the man on the left, "Have you no fear of God?"

Terri felt the question aimed at her. The criminal said something else, but her mind attempted to grasp what she saw.

The man in the center replied, "Today you will be with Me in paradise."

This was Jesus. The Jesus Gramps and Daddy preached about. The Jesus Daddy died for while taking the message to others.

Terri felt as if all eyes were on her, yet no one paid her any attention. Tears gathered in her eyes as people on every side mocked and cursed Jesus.

This is the Son of God, she wanted to shout. *Don't you understand what you're doing?*

Isn't that what you've done? The voice pierced her soul.

Jesus watched her. This was why she felt the center of attention. Their eyes met. She tried to look away but couldn't. *I'm not worthy to be in His presence.*

Love and compassion looked back at her. The moment passed quickly, but for Terri, it seemed an eternity. A moment forever seared into her mind.

Do you doubt Me? I willingly paid the price for your sins. I love you.

She bent over to catch her breath. From a part of her she didn't know still existed, she started to sing. "So I'll cherish the old rugged cross, till my trophies at last I lay down. I will cling to the old rugged cross. And ..."

Why am I singing my response? A memory overcame her. Gramps used to say, "When you sing, you pray twice." He'd used the quote many times in his sermons, fully embracing this teaching by St. Augustine.

This is how much I love you. The words flowed through her like honey.

She straightened and looked at the cross.

Jesus struggled for a breath. "I thirst."

Soldiers soaked a cloth in vinegar and lifted the cloth to his mouth.

Gramps once mentioned in a sermon Jesus refused the drink of the wine to keep a clear mind. His receiving the vinegar fulfilled the Scriptures.

Why did I remember that now?

"Father, into your hands I commit my spirit!" Jesus cried out. With that the earth turned black and shook violently.

Terri reached out for something to hold on to. Nothing was around. She fell to the ground, her body shaking with the earth. When the trembling stopped, she moved closer to Jesus.

Lifeless. Dead. *It is finished.*

She collapsed. A flood of tears erased years of hate and hardness. "I was wrong. Forgive me." She didn't know she had so many tears within her. By the time she stopped, something inside her felt different.

A gentle hand brushed across her body, and she closed her eyes. *I've never felt such love before.* Nothing but darkness surrounded her, yet her heart filled with peace.

When Terri opened her eyes, light had returned. Gabriel stood beside her once again. *I was so caught up in my experience with Jesus, I didn't even notice if Gabriel was there.*

She took Gabriel's hand and wobbled to her feet. "Was that real?"

"Do you believe it was?"

"Yes. I can still feel the earth tremble underneath my feet. I never want to go through another earthquake."

"You experienced that because it was real." Gabriel placed a hand on her shoulder. "Do you believe God loves you?"

"I do. For the first time in a long time. I feel like a different person."

I believe in You, Lord. The God Daddy and Gramps taught me about.

Gabriel kept a steady hand on her arm. "Do you believe Jesus stayed dead?"

"No. I know He rose on the third day. I have no doubt of this truth." The experience with the cross was real, which meant the rest of the Gospels were as well. Jesus rose from the grave after three days. She'd often heard Gramps talk about His appearance to Mary Magdalene, Peter, Thomas, and many others.

She closed her eyes and imagined what it must have felt like to go to the tomb and discover it empty. She could picture the risen Lord appearing to the women. Joy, like nothing she'd known before, rose within her. *When was the last time I felt so free and happy?*

"Why is this happening to me? How is it happening?" She ran a hand over the goose bumps on her arms.

"Do you see the power of prayer? People have been praying for you."

"I think so. I may never understand how this came to be, but I've witnessed the power of prayer. Of God." Gramps had talked about it for years, but she never fully believed it. Now she knew firsthand. Now she believed.

She had so much to comprehend and process. Would she ever understand this experience? *I'll never forget it. Or doubt it.* The light of truth finally dawned. *I made a mistake and allowed hurt and darkness to crowd my life. Instead, I should have allowed light and forgiveness to bring healing.*

Use your new understanding for good. This time, she recognized the voice of Jesus.

Maybe it wasn't too late to change. She thought back over all she'd seen. Scenes from her life. Truth about others and the way her actions impacted them. But one thing made no sense. Hopefully, Gabriel could help.

"I don't understand something."

Gabriel waited patiently. "What is that?"

"Why show me the children at the orphanage? I mean, what can I do? I'm a single woman. How can I help these children?"

Gabriel watched her thoughtfully. "I think you already know the answer."

As she pondered all she had experienced, a hint of an idea formed, but she needed time to think.

The angel placed his other hand on her shoulder. "I want you to remember one thing."

"Okay ..."

"Life is what we make of it. Are you going to waste it or use it for good?"

So many decisions to make. So much to change. Her heart filled with love and joy, yet mystery surrounded her. "Does this mean I'm not dead?"

He stepped back. "You tell me."

"Wait." She had one more request. "Can I see my parents before—" She wasn't sure what she was asking. *Before what? Before I die? Before I live?*

"Some things have to wait." Gabriel's eyes filled with compassion, then he disappeared.

Carol OF THE ROOMS

A new song played through her soul. She'd heard the piece performed when she attended the performance of *Wicked* at the Belk Theater. The words spoke of doing good.

And that's exactly what she planned to do.

MAKING AMENDS

CHAPTER 27

Terri's body propelled through time and space. Some unseen force advanced her in a part-floating-part-walking-part-carried motion. Everything around her became a continuous movement as her surroundings changed. She wasn't sure where she landed, but this wasn't a place she'd been before.

What did Marlee call this place? Purgatory? She wasn't sure.

A bright light appeared ahead. Terri moved toward it. She'd not walked far when she saw her parents. Her heart swelled with love. They looked young. Timeless. *I've not seen them in forty years and can't wait to feel their embrace.* Her eyes watered.

Her parents were not alone. Sophia and Mimi walked alongside them. They motioned with their hands, but she couldn't understand the movement. As she drew closer, they waved for her to go back.

Her heart dropped. *They don't want me.* The old feelings of rejection rose within her. Pain filled her chest. *Even these loved ones don't want me.* "No," she spoke aloud. "I can't allow the darkness to crowd in."

This isn't your time. There is much more for you to do. Learn from what you saw in the rooms, that now-familiar voice spoke to her spirit.

Then a quick message came from her four loved ones. *We love you. We'll see you when the time is right.*

Terri tried to take a step closer but couldn't move. Some unseen force held her in place. *Why is my reflection staring back at me?* Stepping closer, a clear partition appeared between them. No matter how much she wanted to get to her loved ones, she couldn't.

Then suddenly she was propelled backward. Terri felt as if she were being jerked as she spiraled through time and space again. She didn't understand any of this.

Where am I going now?

The constant unknowns and sudden movements were tiresome. Then again, wasn't life that way? More lessons from Gramps crowded her mind. Lessons about loving others more than yourself. There are more important things than money. Serving others is the ultimate form of leadership. And above all, love God with all your heart and soul.

Her mind raced. She became very aware of her senses but unsure of her surroundings. The experience in the rooms and seeing her parents had overwhelmed her. What was to happen now?

Someone spoke, but she couldn't understand what they said. *Who is talking? Where am I?* Struggling to open her eyes, they refused to budge. She tried to move her hand, but something restrained her. *Why can't I move?*

Terri felt lost within herself. Her mind mulled over all she had experienced. *Is any of this real? Am I dreaming? Have I completely lost my mind?*

Her head had a dull pain. Her legs felt irritated. When she attempted to shift them, an intense pain shot through her right leg. Terri's senses gradually returned to a beeping sound every so often. She strained to listen for the direction of the noise.

Soft music played in the background. At first she couldn't make out the lyrics or melody. *Am I still in that unknown place?* She had heard a lot of music there, but it had all been the soundtrack of her life. *Is this also the soundtrack of my life?*

A song began to play she'd not heard in years. She remembered attending Gramps's crusades and hearing the artist sing the song. What was his name? Stan ... Stewart ... Stephen?

That was it, Stephen. No, but close. What was his name? Whoever he was sang the familiar hit "Broken and Spilled Out."

I must still be in that place. But why couldn't she walk and see the way she'd been able to in the rooms? The song changed, but sometime later returned to the same one. Was it a CD playing?

Someone picked up her hand. The rough fingers felt familiar. "Come on, my girl. Come back to me."

Gramps? She strained to listen. It sounded like Gramps. What was he saying, and whom was he talking to? Her heart leaped at his voice. *Will I ever see him again?*

Someone else spoke. "How is she?"

Terri strained to make out the sound. A younger voice. She raced through her memory to place the speaker.

Ethan. Her heart skipped a beat at the realization the voice belonged to Ethan. Then she remembered what she'd done to him. Her heart sank. He would never forgive her for having him fired.

Why does he make my heart skip this way?

Terri couldn't understand the strange feelings within her whenever Ethan came around. She'd never felt this way before.

Chip hadn't made her feel that way, no matter how much she tried to convince herself. James didn't make her heart skip a beat, although she desperately longed for it to. So many years locked away in anger at a man she didn't even love. Not truly. Her heart filled with sadness at the realization she'd only stolen from herself.

Only one other person had caused her heart to beat a little faster and her breath to catch in her chest. She'd not understood because she'd been blinded by her anger. The only other person who made her feel this way had been Mark. A man who'd loved her unconditionally, and she'd not even seen it. The alternative life they could have had …

I can't think about it or I'll go mad.

"Did she just move her finger?" Gramps's breath warmed her neck.

She grabbed what felt like sheets between her fingers. *I'm on a bed?*

"She did move." Hope filled the old man's voice. Commotion sprang up around her, but she couldn't comprehend what was going on.

Time passed in a blur.

The Steve Green song played again. She listened to the words. Something about Jesus being her most precious treasure. Her mind went back to the scene of Jesus on the cross. *I'll never forget what I witnessed. I want Jesus to be my most precious treasure. How can I make that happen? How can I be spilled out and used for Christ?*

Gramps wrapped his fingers around hers.

Whom is he talking to? She focused on the words.

"God, please be with my girl. She's lost and needs You. Help her, Father. Heal her so she can come to know You. I know Your will is perfect, but if she dies now, she will never have the opportunity to make things right. The doctors aren't hopeful, and she's been in this coma for days. I believe You are a God of miracles and will heal my girl. I'm an old man, Lord, and have experienced much loss in my life. I don't know if I can handle losing my girl, especially if she's not made things right with You. You know how many people have prayed for her to turn back to You over the years. She's lost, but she's still very loved."

Terri listened to his prayer. Gramps mentioned a coma. *Is that why everything is so confusing?* Then she cried out to the Lord. *Help me, Lord. I'm broken. You've spilled my life and sins out before me. Let me make things right.* A tear rolled down her cheek. She squeezed Gramps's hand.

Gramps exclaimed, "Praise Jesus!" He patted her hand.

Seconds passed in another blur. She lost all track of time once again.

Open your eyes, a voice whispered to her soul.

She tried, but they wouldn't open. *I can't.* She tried again, but they refused to move.

Try again, the now-familiar voice urged her. A voice so calm and soothing. She felt a great ... what was the word ... peace. Then she remembered where she'd heard the voice before. The voice of Jesus.

A familiar sensation filled her as a hand brushed over her body from head to foot. With one movement, a love like she'd never experienced before passed over her. A love that washed through her body and her heart. She tried to open her eyes again ... and again ...

Until finally ...

Terri opened her eyes and blinked as her grandfather's face came into view.

CHAPTER 28

"She's awake!" Gramps yelled from her bedside.

Doctors and nurses rushed in. Terri had never been poked and prodded so much. After a while, she grew annoyed.

"Thank you, God," Gramps prayed aloud from the corner the medical staff had relegated him to.

Tears blurred her vision. She thought back to when she'd been a little girl and grew excited whenever Gramps returned home from a trip. She'd sit at his feet for hours and listen as he shared his experiences. That feeling of love and belonging was how she felt now. Her mind went to the numerous stories Gramps had shared, especially those of people who had been lost but now were found. They were blind but now could see. Peace filled her again.

I can relate. Now it's my story.

She attempted to speak, but something prevented her from saying anything. The doctor explained she had to be intubated. Terri had a lot to say, but she could wait. In the meantime, she was thankful to be alive and content to listen to the soothing words of her grandfather.

A day later, the doctor removed the tube but said it would take a few days before Terri could speak.

Aunt Maggie and Aunt Beth visited her, along with her cousins. They all spoke kindly to her and expressed gratefulness she was awake and would recover.

Not that I deserve their kindness. They've shown me more grace than I've ever given anyone. Her mind focused on the song playing throughout her soul. *Amazing Grace, how sweet the sound. That saved a wretch like me.*

While convalescing, Terri watched the Alastair Sim version of *A Christmas Carol*. She thought through her experiences in the white rooms and what a wretch she'd been. Her dreams had been a lot like *A Christmas Carol. Were the rooms real?* Then she wondered how long it was until Christmas.

Things were different for Scrooge, who walked, danced around, and revealed the change within him. She lay stuck in this hospital bed, limited by the ability of her body. Yet she embraced this time of being still to mull over her experience. It gave her time to think and pray about the life she wanted to live and the changes she would need to make.

"What ... what happened?" she asked once she could speak.

"You were in a severe car accident. Your car crashed into a tree," Gramps said. He had never left her bedside. "They had to cut you out of the vehicle. Your right leg, now in a cast, is broken."

"How bad was it?" Terri didn't want to ask but needed to know. "Did I die?"

Gramps fidgeted, refusing to meet her eyes. "The car behind you saw the accident and called 911. If someone had not summoned help immediately, you would not have survived." His voice became thick with emotion. "We almost lost you." He picked up her hand. "You nearly died at the scene of the accident and again at the hospital. Both times, you had to be revived."

Terri took a while to process the information. She said little but wondered again about Christmas. Watching the movie on TV, she realized the holiday must be quickly approaching. "Gramps, when is Christmas?" Her voice still sounded raspy.

His mouth dropped. "In three days. Why?"

A smile played on her lips as ideas filled her head. "Just curious."

The doctor visited later and said he'd like to keep her another day for observation but promised to have her home by Christmas. Because of her broken leg, she could not put any pressure on it—which meant she couldn't go home alone.

She had decisions to make about where to go and how to care for herself as she healed.

Terri pulled herself up in bed. "I owe you both an apology."

Her aunts spun around. They stood at the foot of her hospital bed as disbelief filled their faces.

"I've behaved terribly over the years. I'm so sorry."

She didn't know who cried harder. Then she glanced at the corner where Gramps kept vigil. He beamed through his tears.

"We had some good times together when I was a child." She'd blocked out these memories until the spirit unveiled her past. "I have a favor to ask."

Her aunts shared a look of trepidation.

"Anything." Aunt Maggie cast a wary glance at her sister.

Terri suppressed a grin. "I'd like for all of us to spend Christmas day together." Her aunts' mouths dropped open. "Of course, I want your families with us. I can't cook, but I'll arrange to have everything catered."

"No," Beth and Maggie spoke in unison. "We'll cook." They were adamant. This was the first family Christmas they would spend together in over two decades.

The rest of the visit revolved around making plans for Terri to go home with Gramps the following day and what they would serve for Christmas dinner. It didn't take long to decide on the traditional Southern favorites. Turkey and dressing with giblet gravy. Macaroni and cheese. Sweet potato casserole. Green bean casserole. Deviled eggs. Squash casserole. Carrot cake. And of course, the pies—pecan, pumpkin, apple, and her favorite, lemon meringue.

Terri explained to her aunts Abigail had already arranged for home health to visit Gramps several times a week. They would assist both Terri and Gramps until she got back on her feet. Terri couldn't remember the last time she laughed. It reminded her how much she used to enjoy her aunts' company. *How could I have been so blind for so long?*

As her aunts prepared to leave, she stopped them. "Can you help me with one more favor?"

CHAPTER 29

Gramps waited until they arrived home, both settled into recliners in his living room before he spoke. "What happened to you?"

Terri grabbed his hand. "You wouldn't believe me if I told you." Her heart had never been so full.

He leaned back in his recliner and folded his hands. "Try me."

For the next two hours, Terri shared everything, starting with her encounter with Marlee. She shared Gabriel's visits and the journey with the three spirits, ending with her watching Jesus die on the cross. Told about seeing her parents, Sophia, and Mimi. By the time she finished, Gramps's handkerchief had to be wrung out from all the tears.

"Do you believe what you witnessed is real?" His voice choked.

"I do." She had a frog in her own throat.

"Have you made things right?"

"I'm not sure." Terri never took her eyes from his. "I asked for God's forgiveness while I was in the coma. I could still hear and think, but my body limited me from moving or talking to others, except in my heart." They sat in companionable silence for a few moments, then the realization struck her like a semi. "I need to say it out loud."

Gramps squeezed her hand. "Would you like me to lead you?"

Terri exchanged a look of adoration with him. How many times had she watched Gramps lead someone to Christ? She shook her head. "I know what to say."

Gramps beamed as she bowed her head.

"Father God, I'm a sinner. I've allowed years of hurt and hatred to build up in my heart. I've been mean and hurtful to others in return. Thank You for revealing all my shortcomings to me. Please forgive my sins. I love You and want You to live in my heart. In Jesus's name." She kept her head bowed a long time, basking in the moment and time in God's presence.

A song rose within her. From her soul, it moved to her heart, past her throat, until she opened her mouth. The song burst forth and she sang. *Yes, Jesus loves me. Yes, Jesus loves me. Yes, Jesus loves me, for He told me so.*

When she looked up, Gramps wiped away another round of tears. "He told me He loves me." Her heart jumped at the memory. "I saw firsthand when He hung on the cross."

Gramps bowed his head. "Thank You, God."

"Are you able to do one more baptism?" Terri surprised herself as the words came tumbling out. "You baptized me as a child, and I want you to baptize me again. Maybe everyone doesn't want or need a second baptism, but after the way I've lived over the last two decades, I need this symbolic rebirth."

He squeezed her hand before letting go. "I think we can figure something out." Love and pride shone in his eyes.

Carol OF THE ROOMS

Several hours later, Terri glanced up from her reading, marking the Bible passage with her finger. "You and Ethan were discussing the Damascus Road experience when I arrived one day." Her fingers nervously tapped the page.

Gramps looked up from his own Bible and waited for her to continue.

"You both prayed I would have such an experience." She stopped to take a breath. "Your prayers were answered."

Gramps gave her the time she needed to gather her thoughts. She'd been like Saul. He persecuted believers and even stood nearby, approving when Stephen was stoned. After God revealed himself to Saul on the Damascus Road, he became a believer. At some point thereafter he became known by his Greek name of Paul and preached the gospel all over the known world.

Terri had done much the same thing. She'd persecuted those who cared for her most. It was time to apologize. Marlee had been right. She needed to live for others, not herself. *I have some thinking and planning to do.*

"Gramps, I have some amends to make."

CHAPTER 30

May Patterson glanced around the table at the children seated in a circle. She could do nothing more with the sparse donations they'd received. The situation broke her heart.

Alexander turned to Mia. "Here, let's share." His thoughtfulness touched May. These children did not understand how much they missed out on and were thankful for the little they had.

She'd prepared blueberry pancakes, eggs, and sausage for the children's breakfast. Someone had donated a turkey, which she would serve at lunch, along with two sides. How she'd love to prepare a feast for the children, but to them, what she served would be a banquet.

Her fundraising efforts had raised enough to purchase all the children a sweater and pair of socks. They needed so much more, including blankets and shoes.

"That's mine," one child protested as another took the last piece of sausage.

"Now children." May waited patiently. She was about to explain the importance of sharing when a knock sounded on the door. *Who could that be?*

Alexander hopped up from the table and ran to answer the door.

"It's Santa Claus!" The children jumped from their chairs and ran to the jolly man.

May's mouth dropped open.

"Ho. Ho. Ho." Santa didn't wait for an invitation to enter. "I come bearing gifts." A red bag bulging with presents had been draped over his shoulder.

"From whom? Who would provide such a charitable act?" No one came to mind.

His eyes twinkled. "A benefactor who wishes to remain anonymous."

The children gathered around Santa. Each girl received a baby doll and Barbie, while each boy received a car and train. There were clothes, including shoes, and a blanket for each child. Every little face lit up with delight and amazement.

"Where did all this come from?" May asked. "Who would have done this?"

Santa handed her an envelope. "This is for food."

May accepted the gift certificate and gasped at the amount. It was enough to last at least three months. She grinned at Santa. "This is too good to be true."

Santa held up a finger. "One more thing." He handed her another note, stating the heat would be turned back on later that day.

"On Christmas Day? How did someone—" She inhaled sharply. Their electricity, water bill, and other expenses were taken care of for the next year. She covered her face as a wave of emotion overcame her. She dropped to her knees, overwhelmed by this miracle. "Thank you, Lord." God had more than come through. She'd been praying for a way to provide for these children but never imagined anything this amazing. She'd scraped by for years and barely made ends meet. Now God had shown up in a big way. He more than provided for these precious children. "Bless whoever our benefactor may be, Lord."

She watched the children play with their toys and cherished the happiness on each of their faces. A wave of love and adoration washed through her heart for these precious souls entrusted to her care—and for the generosity of her benefactor.

"Merry Christmas." Abigail gently shook Timmy awake.

He rolled over. His smile seemed brighter than a Christmas tree.

"I have blueberry muffins."

His eyes twinkled. Her son loved blueberry muffins for breakfast.

Before she finished getting Timmy up, showered, and dressed, her mom appeared. "You have a visitor."

"Who?" She couldn't imagine who would visit her on Christmas morning.

"You'll see. I'll finish with Timmy." Mom patted her arm. There wasn't much left, and the remaining task would not take long. After explaining where she was in the morning routine, she excused herself, thankful Mom was able and willing to take over.

Abigail walked to the back and opened the sliding glass door. *Why is a delivery man here? And on Christmas Day.* "May I help you?" She crossed her arms, figuring he must have the wrong address.

"Are you Abigail Walker?" He checked his clipboard. "I have a delivery for you."

"I think you're mistaken." She'd not ordered anything.

The man confirmed her name and address again.

"Who is it from? Is this some type of joke?"

The man read the card. "It says 'Santa Claus.'"

Abigail burst into laughter. She had no choice but to play along and see what transpired. Moving aside, she motioned the delivery man in. Mom and Timmy appeared and took a seat on the sofa to watch the transaction.

The delivery man began carrying boxes inside. Opening the presents, Abigail found three boxes of food. Then a TV. A recliner. Clothes. Even toys for Timmy. She looked from her mom to the delivery man. "Who did this? Who would send all these gifts? And why?"

The delivery man turned to leave. "The bed will be here Thursday."

"What bed?"

He cast her a strange look. "The hospital bed."

Abigail sank onto the floor while emotion wracked her body at the generosity of a stranger. An hour later, her mood changed when the phone rang.

Terri Neely's voice held a hint of urgency. "I need you today."

Abigail scowled at the phone she held, her festive spirit ruined. "It's Christmas Day. Can't I have one day with my family?"

"Be here at five o'clock sharp."

Abigail opened her mouth to object. Then closed it. *I'm a prisoner to my job. Maybe it's time to find something else.* She wrote down the directions her boss provided. "Can't it wait until tomorrow?" She bit her tongue. Even she had her limits. Abigail looked over at Timmy lying on the couch and remembered what was most important. Providing for him.

"One more thing," her boss said. "I'd like for you to bring your family."

Carol OF THE ROOMS

Abigail blinked and stared at the phone again. *Did I hear her correctly?*

"You won't believe it." Emma turned to her husband after hanging up the phone. He lowered the paper and watched her.

"I just received a call from—" The doorbell interrupted her. She held her hand up to assure her husband she would get the door. Their guests wouldn't arrive for another two hours, and she'd been preparing Christmas lunch for two days.

A delivery man stood on her doorstep. "For you."

Emma's mouth gaped open when the deliveryman held up a twenty-pound turkey. She could never get this thing cooked in time for their guest. The delivery man pointed to the tag. It had already been cooked, and she inhaled the juicy aroma. "Who is it from?"

"Someone who loves you very much." The delivery man tipped his hat and turned toward his truck. He made two more trips with boxes. Emma and Derrick exchanged looks of disbelief. The generosity overwhelmed them as they unwrapped the presents.

The phone call from earlier slipped her mind as she rushed to finish preparations. Their guests would be here soon.

Derrick walked into the kitchen to assist her sometime later. "What were you going to tell me earlier? Who was on the phone?"

The doorbell rang again, and Emma went to answer it. She peeked through the sheer curtains beside the door at their guests. She looked forward to a wonderful time together and playing word games after lunch. But most of all, she looked forward to the invitation she'd received from Terri for tonight. With her hand on the doorknob, her friends and in-laws waiting on the other side, she turned back to her husband. "Aunt Ri. She invited us to supper."

CHAPTER 31

"You're late." Terri scowled from her seat, her foot propped up beside the kitchen table.

Abigail felt a knot in her gut. "I'm sorry. After all, it is Christmas Day." *Why can't she ever be pleased?*

Terri broke into a smile, which reached all the way to her eyes. "Merry Christmas."

Abigail's mouth dropped open. She'd never seen her boss look so joyful. "What?" *This isn't anything like the person I know. Who is this woman?* She had seemed different on the two quick visits Abigail had made since the accident, but this ...

Terri pushed herself up from the table, leaned on her crutches, and with the help of her caregiver, hobbled over to her employee.

"Merry Christmas." Terri hugged Abigail, then hobbled over to Timmy and pulled him into a hug.

Abigail didn't know how to respond. "I don't understand." *None of this makes sense. She demanded I come over and bring my family. Now, she wishes us a Merry Christmas ...*

"We have much to talk about." Terri motioned toward the buffet prepared on the kitchen counters. "After we eat."

Terri called everyone to join them. "I know you're all hungry, so I'll keep this short." She glanced around the room. Many nodded. "I've treated you all horribly over the years, and I don't deserve your forgiveness. A lot happened after my car accident. Most of what occurred is too unbelievable to go into at the moment." Her eyes searched the room.

Gramps winked his encouragement.

"What I want to say is I'm sorry. Truly sorry."

A collective gasp filled the room.

"God showed me the error of my ways, and I've gotten my heart right with Him. After this cast comes off my leg, Gramps will baptize me. I wanted to apologize and say I love you all."

Everyone talked at once. Uncertain looks shifted to smiling faces. A few people stepped forward to make room for more to enter the cramped kitchen quarters. It took a while to quiet the group for the blessing.

Gramps blessed the food. Then he thanked God for the miracle in Terri's heart and life.

As she bowed her head, Terri caught the eye of her niece, who looked so much like Sophia. Emma's eyes danced with merriment, and her hair fell below her shoulders like her mother's. A pang rose in Terri's heart at how much she missed her best friend. She'd buried so many emotions under the anger she'd carried for too long.

"Oh, Aunt Ri!" Emma made a beeline to her the moment Gramps finished the blessing. The girl she'd hated for so long now caused her heart to overflow with love.

After everyone finished eating, Terri hobbled to the piano. She'd not played in years and wasn't sure how much she remembered, but she had to try. With her foot in a cast, she struggled to find a posture that worked but refused to let her malady deter her. Finally, she shifted into a position where she could play.

"Joy to the world, the Lord is come ..."

Before she finished the first verse, the family gathered around. Terri couldn't maintain her stance long. Thankfully, Emma slid onto the bench and picked up where she left off. Sophia would be so proud of her daughter.

For the next hour, the family bonded over Christmas carols. The spirit had been right when she said these were songs of joy.

Nervously pulling at her fingers, Abigail sat on the sofa beside Terri's chair.

Terri turned to her. "I owe you an apology for so many things." Her gaze fell on Timmy, who played checkers with Gramps. "Things will be different."

"Ooo ... kay." Abigail drew the word out, unsure what to say.

"First, I'm giving you a raise." She named a sum, causing Abigail to whistle. Her salary would more than triple.

"Also, no more overtime."

Abigail held up a hand in protest. "But—"

"There's little that can't wait until regular business hours. Spending time with Timmy and your parents is more important."

"I—"

"Would you still like to be an architect?"

Abigail sucked in a sharp breath. "Of course. More than anything." *It'll never happen.*

"We can discuss a solution so I can mentor you. When you're ready, we'll work you into an apprenticeship."

Abigail readjusted her red and green scarf with shaky hands. "But—"

"Don't worry. With your raise, you shouldn't struggle. If you do, let me know. I'll do whatever I can to help," she spoke rapidly. "I'll even pay for you to go back to college."

Abigail cried out in delight, "This is too good to be true!"

Terri studied her. "That reminds me. One more thing." Terri turned her attention back to Abigail's son. "As for Timmy ..."

Abigail straightened as her eyes darted to the boy. "What about my son?"

"I'm going to pay for his surgery."

Abigail almost hyperventilated. Sobs of happiness and relief wracked her body. *This is too much. Thank You, Lord. Thank You.*

Terri waited, giving Abigail time to process the news.

Her assistant clapped her hands together. "Thank You, Lord." Tears fell. A look of confusion overcame her, then her eyes lit up. "It was you. You're Santa Claus."

Terri didn't acknowledge the statement. *Abigail has been a trooper over the years. It's time I show her how grateful I am. No one else would have ever stuck with me this long.*

"I need your help with a few things." *Remember, don't let your left hand know what your right hand is doing.* "Especially while I'm convalescing, but we can discuss that tomorrow. After all, it's Christmas Day. We should spend this time with our families." She held up her eggnog in salute.

Carol OF THE ROOMS

After Abigail returned to her family, Terri noticed she was singing. But it wasn't a Christmas carol that sprang forth from her soul. No, it was a very different song. This one she regretted not being able to sing when she performed in *The Sound of Music*. That solo went to the Mother Abbess. A song about climbing mountains, reaching for dreams, and never giving up.

In that moment, one thing became clear. The soundtrack of her life continued.

CHAPTER 32

Terri called this meeting but didn't know what to expect. She nervously wrung her hands while she waited. The last week had been hectic, but Abigail had more than proved her worth by helping out during her convalescence.

Terri wouldn't trade this time for anything. She spent a lot of time studying her Bible, which led to in-depth conversations with Gramps. She loved their time together and cherished every moment. After all, Gramps turned ninety this year, and only God knew how much more time they would have together.

A knock sounded on the door, and her aunt opened it. Terri nodded at her guest when he arrived. He looked thinner and had stubble on his chin but still took her breath away.

"Terri?" Uncertainty filled his voice.

"Have a seat." She gave a reassuring smile as she pointed to a nearby chair. "I guess it surprised you to hear from me?"

He crossed his arms and stood with his feet apart. "You could say that."

"Ethan, I ..." She faltered as uncertainty filled her voice.

A look of uneasiness crossed his face, and his gaze shot silent questions her way.

"Were you at the hospital after my accident?"

He stared at his feet. "Yes, but how—"

"I thought I heard you." A lump formed in her throat.

Ethan jumped as if jolted by lightning. "You were in a coma."

"I know." They maintained an uncomfortable silence. Terri took another deep breath. *Help me, Lord.* She shifted slightly for a better look at her guest. "I owe you an apology, Ethan. A big one."

His eyes widened, but he remained silent.

"I was wrong. I hope you can find it in your heart to forgive me."

Ethan stared at her. His jaw tightened until his teeth ground against one another, but he eventually nodded. "I forgive you." Sincerity shone back at her.

"Thank you." She shifted again. "There's something I have to know. You prayed for me?" The question sounded more like an accusation than she meant, but she had to be sure.

He clasped his hands behind his back. "I did."

"Why?" Her leg throbbed until she repositioned it.

His voice held a strong conviction. "Because you needed it."

She thought about all the conversations she'd walked in on as he and Gramps discussed the Bible. "You're right. I did." *Okay, Lord, where do we go from here?*

Ethan watched her.

"Thank you for praying."

"We're told to love our enemies." His eyes narrowed. "Why did you do it?" Hurt edged into his voice. He'd finally asked the question she'd been dreading.

Terri held his gaze. "The truth?"

"Of course." He tapped his foot on the floor.

Terri didn't want to admit the truth, but they needed to have this conversation. "I enjoyed our time together but—"

Ethan shot her a look of disbelief and shoved his hands in the pockets of his jeans. "So that's why—"

"It surprised me to discover I was thinking of you. At home. On a jobsite. Even in the office, you kept coming to mind." *What else can I say? How do I explain my actions when, in retrospect, they were selfish?* "I was scared, Ethan. It felt like you haunted my mind." Terri bowed her head in embarrassment. "And heart."

"So, you had me fired because you had feelings for me?" Disbelief filled his voice.

She nodded. "I'm so sorry."

"I forgive you." He slowly let out a breath. "Only God knows what we might have had together."

Terri cleared her throat. "How can you forgive me so easily? And quickly?"

He refused to meet her gaze. "Because I forgave you long ago. I knew it came from a hurting heart."

"You make forgiveness look so easy."

He looked at her then. "Forgiveness is a choice for me. Besides, didn't Jesus teach that we should turn the other cheek when others hurt us—especially people we care about?"

Terri straightened at the realization Ethan had the same deep feelings. She'd been kidding herself in thinking his interest had only been mild curiosity when he mentioned the idea of asking her out to Gramps.

He took a step closer. "I'd heard the stories about you but didn't believe them."

"What stories?" She felt silly asking. She *knew* what stories.

"How selfish and self-centered you were."

Her reputation preceded her, and she hadn't cared. She'd walked around dead inside for so long and didn't even know it.

"Then I saw the way you love and dote on your grandfather." Ethan stared at a photo of Gramps and Mimi on the wall. "I saw something underneath that tough exterior."

"You were the only one." Other than her grandfather, who always saw good in her.

"I knew if anyone could love Gramps the way you did"—his lips turned up slightly— "they couldn't be all bad. You had more to give than you realized. Someone just needed to unlock your heart."

"You ..." She couldn't finish the sentence. Her heart pounded. *This is overwhelming.* Terri forced herself to take another breath. "Felt the same?"

"Yes."

He looked like a wounded animal, and Terri realized how much her actions had destroyed.

"We could have had something special." He looked at the floor again.

"I'm sorry." *More than I ever thought possible. Plenty of time later to think about the what-might-have-beens. I think there's even a song similar to that idea. I'll have to look it up. Why am I not surprised?*

Ethan rolled his shoulders. "I believe you are."

Terri swallowed. She had to ask. Regardless of the answer, she would always have regret if she didn't. "Is it too late? For us?"

Ethan leaned against the wall and continued to stare at the floor while kicking the carpet. His face tightened and then relaxed some. When he finally looked at her, sadness filled his eyes. "I think so."

Carol OF THE ROOMS

"May I ask why?"

"You hurt me. Deeply." The sharpness of the words stung. "Although I forgave you, I'm not sure I could ever trust you again. I'd always wonder ..."—he exhaled and looked away— "when you'd hurt me again."

No one will ever want you. They'll remember the way you used to treat them. Terri struggled to drown out the negative thoughts. "I've changed."

Ethan pushed himself away from the wall. "I believe you have. The woman who sent me away would never have apologized. Maybe in another place and time." He shook his head. "But not now. Not here."

No one waited forever. Mark had proven that fact on her journey through the rooms. He'd waited longer than anyone should, but eventually even he gave up on her.

I can do all things through him who strengthens me. She closed her eyes and drew comfort from Philippians 4:13.

She didn't blame Ethan for not trusting her. If the tables were turned, she would probably react the same way. The revelation made her more determined than ever to keep changing. To let her actions speak for her heart. Terri wanted to be like Scrooge and be better than her word. She felt as if she'd seen every version ever made of *A Christmas Carol* since coming home from the hospital. She'd also read through the classic three times. Okay, maybe she'd become a little obsessed with the story in the past week. After all, the old miser had become as good a friend, as good a master—or boss—and as good a man as the old city had ever known. She wanted to follow in his footsteps and be the same way. If Scrooge could change, then she could change as well.

Then an idea struck her. Why hadn't she thought about it before? "Ethan, is there someone else?"

He shrugged. "My aunt set me up on a blind date. This weekend." He turned his eyes away from her.

"But?"

"I've also become close friends with someone at work. I don't know if anything will happen, but I—"

"You need to find out." Just as she wished she'd given Mark a chance. *How could I have been so dense?* When it came to relationships, she seemed to make one faux pas after another. At least, she had Gramps. However, he was ninety and wouldn't be with her forever. She had some thinking to do. "I wish you all the best. I hope you find what you're looking for."

"Now I know you've changed." Ethan smiled—an easygoing grin—for the first time.

"Guess I have." She grinned back. In more ways than he'd ever know. Would he believe her if she told him what happened? Now didn't feel like the time or place to share such a crazy story. "Gramps misses you. I hope you'll stay in touch with him."

"I will."

Terri had a feeling they had maintained contact this entire time. "He's in his office if you would like to see him."

Ethan stepped forward with an extended hand. "Friends?"

"Friends." She held his gaze and then shook his palm.

He reached around and gave her a quick hug but didn't linger. He then excused himself, went to his car, and quickly returned holding out a bag. "There's only one. May I?"

Terri laughed. "Chocolate-covered and cream-filled?"

"Of course. Gramps wouldn't have any other type of donut."

"Just one." She held her finger up. "Tell him to enjoy."

"I will." Ethan flashed her a smile and headed down the hall.

Carol OF THE ROOMS

Once alone, Terri buried her face in her hands and cried. *My selfish actions affected so many people. How could I have been so blind?*

Laughter drifted down the hallway. She bowed her head in prayer. "Thank You for helping me make things right."

That's the first step. I'm proud of you. There are more to come. I will never leave you nor forsake you. God continued speaking to her, prompting her to keep making amends.

She needed to do one more thing to make amends with Ethan. He had a job at the hospital now, but she felt the importance of doing this. If nothing else, at least his employment record could be expunged of her actions, and he'd have his good name restored. She needed to rescind her complaint to the agency.

"Thank you for coming." Terri stood as her guest entered the living room the following day. She propped herself on her crutches, realizing how stressful making amends could be.

The woman squared her shoulders, obviously ready for a fight. "I'm here."

"You have every right to be angry." Terri kept her voice steady.

Victoria Nelson paced the room. "You are a selfish lady. Thinking only of yourself." Her eyes darkened.

Terri nodded. "You're right. I have been."

"So, why am I here?" Victoria snapped.

Terri pointed to the seat next to her. "Please sit."

Victoria took a step back. "I'd rather stand."

"Then I'll come to the point."

"Please do." Victoria's tone felt like a sharp knife blade.

Terri squeezed the handgrips on her crutches. "I owe you an apology."

"What?" The woman stared at her in surprise.

"Everything you said is true. I have been selfish. I thought only of myself. I didn't care how my actions affected others." These things were hard but necessary to admit.

Victoria opened her mouth, then closed it.

Terri gave her a few minutes. "How's the weather been?" She decided on a safe subject matter. She'd been sequestered indoors at Gramps's for the last few weeks as her leg healed and hadn't paid any attention to the weather report.

They visited for a short time. Then Victoria took a step closer. "What happened to you?" Before Terri could say anything, the woman took the seat she'd refused earlier.

"I'm not sure you'd believe me if I told you." She'd not worried about telling Gramps, but would others believe her? Or think her crazy?

"Try me." Victoria shifted in her chair.

Terri adjusted her own position and pulled in a quick breath. "I died."

Victoria's mouth fell open. "What?"

"When I had my accident. I died." Terri hesitated, searching for a starting place. "I entered a room full of bright light, which made everything appear white. In the room, I met the angel Gabriel."

Victoria scooted back in her seat. "The one in the Bible?"

"Yes. The very one." Terri told her about visiting three rooms where she saw her past, present, and future. "While there, I heard the soundtrack of my life. The music revealed the color of my soul at that moment. I'd not realized how much certain people and experiences had affected me."

"So you really died?" Victoria stared at her as if she couldn't decide whether to believe what she was hearing or not. "What else did you see?"

This was the craziest part of all. Would she believe it? "After seeing the future ahead and what would happen if I continued on my current path, I felt as if I were moving through time. The next thing I saw was ..."

Victoria rubbed her hands together in obvious anticipation. "Yes?"

"I saw a hill and three men hanging on a wooden cross." Terri watched for a reaction.

"You mean Jesus? I've heard they crucified Him, and He rose from the grave, but it sounded so absurd." Victoria's eyes fell on a picture of Jesus on the wall.

"He did. I saw Jesus for myself as the soldiers raised a sponge with vinegar on it. Jesus told me He loved me enough to die for my sins." Tears now filled Terri's eyes. She could see the scene as vividly as when she'd been there. "He loved me, even when no one else did. He loved me even when I didn't deserve it. Jesus is the only person who could cleanse my heart, forgive my sins, and make me whiter than snow."

Victoria's eyes widened in surprise. "So, Jesus is why you're so changed?"

"He is the only reason." Terri searched the woman's face. "Do you know Jesus?" *I can't believe I asked. When is the last time I was that bold?*

Victoria seemed to ponder the question. "I thought so, but now I'm not so sure."

Terri scooted toward the front of her chair. "Why?"

"I've gone through the motions of asking for God's help when things go wrong. I don't have a relationship like you explained." She stared at her hands resting in her lap. "I guess I've thought of Him like a genie who would appear and make everything right when I needed it."

"And did He?"

Victoria shook her head. "No."

"Would you like to have a living relationship with Jesus?" Terri reached for the woman's hand.

Victoria didn't answer right away. Her forehead creased. "I would."

"Then repeat this after me." Terri closed her eyes. "God, I'm a sinner. I want to know You and have a relationship with You. Please forgive me of my sins. I want You to live within me. Change me to be the woman You would have me to be. Amen."

Victoria's eyes watered after repeating the prayer. "What now?"

"Here's a Bible." Terri handed her the one she'd been reading, along with a tissue. "Now you need to find a Bible-believing church."

"Then I'll have a relationship with God?"

"It takes work, but if you stay in His Word and fellowship with other believers, that's the beginning of growth." Terri placed a hand over Victoria's. "One more thing. I've rescinded my complaints to the Better Business Bureau and Interior Design Association." She hated to admit it, but Victoria had been right in her design. After studying the pictures again, Terri realized she liked Victoria's design better than her own. She had plans for the two of them to work together again—if Victoria agreed.

CHAPTER 33

Terri sought out her assistant in the drawing room. "Is everything ready?"

Abigail handed her the final designs she'd been working on. "I think so."

Over the last few weeks, Terri had given her assistant more responsibility and been impressed with how quickly the younger woman had caught on to her additional duties. Abigail had always been a hard worker, but with a greater investment, she seemed to work even harder than before.

Terri picked up the plans and looked at them before placing them back on the table. She repeated the action three times. "Do you think ..."

Abigail handed her the phone. "You won't know if you don't ask."

Terri took it and punched in the number. She wasted no time when May Patterson answered. "This is Terri Neely. Do you still need help with renovations?" She could not get the orphans out of her mind. They haunted her.

"Yes. We do." The woman sounded flabbergasted.

"I'd like to meet with you." Terri got to the point, and the women set up a meeting for the following week. "And one more thing. Would you bring a few children with you?"

May coughed. "Are ... are you sure?"

"Yes. I'd like to meet them." Terri purposely didn't ask for anyone in particular. *Will the children from the rooms be there? It's in Your hands, Lord.*

Terri and Abigail worked steadily on ideas and projects over the course of the week in preparation for the upcoming meeting. They had plans on how to improve the orphanage and meet all the needs shared on that initial visit when Terri had shown May Patterson unceremoniously to the door.

May arrived ten days later with several children from the orphanage. Two of the children she brought with her were Mia and Alexander.

What are You trying to tell me, Lord?

Terri pulled up a chair. Her leg was out of the cast, but she now wore a brace. Earlier in the week, she had begun physical therapy to regain the use of her leg. She looked back and forth between the children, making eye contact with each one. "Hello. My name is Terri. I hope Ms. Patterson and I will be able to work together to make where you live a better place for all of you."

You're going to have to help me, Lord. Show me what to do.

Mia's eyes widened with delight. "I've seen you."

"Really? Where?" *Did Mia see me in the rooms?*

"In my dreams. You were watching over me." Mia glanced uncertainly at Alexander, who narrowed his eyes at Terri.

"Hopefully, we're destined to become friends." Terri led the children to a nearby table where she had snacks laid out. She listened as they told her about living at the orphanage and the improvements they would like. As they spoke, she made notes.

Abigail returned a few moments later and introduced them to Timmy. He and Alexander quickly became friends.

It took every ounce of self-control for Terri to pull herself away from the children and return to business. She showed May the plans she had drawn up for improvements.

May dabbed at her eyes with a tissue. "How can I ever thank you?"

"Well,"—Terri pulled her further back into the room and lowered her voice— "what is the story with Mia and Alexander?"

"Both of their parents are gone. They were raised by their grandparents until they couldn't care for the children any longer."

"Are they still alive?"

May shook her head. "No. They died within weeks of one another."

"My grandfather is ninety. Maybe ..." Terri's mind ran one hundred miles an hour. This wasn't something that could be rushed. She forced herself to breathe and slow her racing heart. "Would it be possible for me to spend time with them? Get to know them better?"

May looked over her shoulder at the children. "My goal is to see these children loved, but ..." Uncertainty filled her eyes. Terri didn't blame the woman for not trusting her yet. "I don't want to see them hurt."

"Me, neither." Terri placed a hand on her arm. "We'll take this slow. I won't take a step without talking with you."

May narrowed her eyes. "What happened to you?"

Terri laughed. "Not sure you'd believe me if I told you." At times, she didn't believe it herself.

Terri smiled as she opened the door. She'd picked the children up that morning and brought them to visit Gramps. Over the past few months, they had both become attached to Mia and Alexander.

"You are my sunshine ..." Gramps sang with the children.

Terri remembered sitting on his lap as a little girl while he sang the song to her. She often found Gramps singing with the children, telling them stories, or playing games. They kept him young. Even Aunt Beth and Aunt Maggie were taken with the young people and enjoyed finding reasons to bring their grandchildren for a visit.

Mia giggled as Gramps launched into a story, and Alexander listened intently. She'd been the same way at their age. They had so much in common. They'd found love and happiness with Gramps when their own parents and grandparents had been taken from them.

Terri stepped forward when Gramps finished his story. "Why don't you go see what snacks Aunt Beth may have for you?"

"Afterward, can we take pictures?" Alexander had picked up her interest in photography.

"Of course." She tousled his hair as the children headed into the kitchen. Then she hurried toward Gramps.

"You won't believe it." She still couldn't wrap her mind around the news. After making renovations to the orphanage, they served as nothing more than a bandage. "The house they are in may last two or three more years, but even that will be pushing it. It is terribly out of date and more dilapidated than I ever imagined." Terri sat beside him. "I've called in every favor I can think of and then some."

"Yes, you've told me."

She rubbed her hands together. "The news gets even better." *It's got to be You, Lord? I can't wait to see what You're doing.*

"Are you going to keep me waiting all day?" Gramps pulled her out of her daydream.

"Sorry. Woolgathering." She'd been doing a lot of that lately. "May and I met with Ray Peterson. He offered us a tract of land. Ray bought it late last year. Told us, 'I have no plans for it, other than God laid it on my heart to buy the land.'"

Gramps grinned. "The Lord is showing us time and again He has his hand on this situation. How large is it? An acre?"

Terri grabbed his hand. "It's twelve acres, and more land around it is for sale."

Gramps let out a low whistle.

"He took us to look at it. It's perfect." She pulled out her camera and showed him the pictures. She never dreamed God would open the doors in such a marvelous way.

"Looks like you're going to be busy." Gramps eyes twinkled. "I think you'll keep Abigail and Victoria hustling as well."

Terri laughed. "That's a fact." She and Victoria had been working together on numerous projects. She'd called the woman earlier, and the designer promised to decorate the new facility. They'd worked to build a friendship over the last few months, and Victoria often joined her and Abigail for a weekly Bible study.

Alexander jumped down from the step-up into the kitchen. "Can we go outside now?"

"Sure. Let's go." Terri reached for her shawl to protect her from the April winds. She loved being able to keep up with the children now that her leg was finally back to normal.

Gramps reached for his cane and followed them outside as she gave the children some pointers. When she took a seat beside him on the porch swing, his face lit up as he watched the children.

Terri patted his knee. "The children are so good for both of us. Maybe we should contact a local nursing home. May told me how good it is for the children to be around older adults. I bet the same is true for them." She spoke faster and faster, tapping her hands on the swing's armrest. "Think about all we do together. Read, garden, take pictures, make crafts, sing, listen to your stories, play games—"

"Take a breath. It's a great idea. I love it, and I'm sure others will as well." He reached for her hand and squeezed it. "Slow down." Gramps always had a way of grounding her when those creative juices became overwhelming—at least for everyone else.

"I'll have to look into some local nursing homes." She thought about the rooms—she had no other way to explain her experience—where she'd seen the older people. She'd not understood why at the time, but maybe this was the reason, to bring them together with these children.

Gramps set the swing in motion. "A couple of my friends are at a nearby facility. I'll get you the information."

Terri handed Dani, the activities director at a nearby nursing home, a plastic cup, then poured punch into it. When she and May had reached out, Dani had been excited about having the children visit.

After the party, Alexander set up a checkers game, and Mia went to talk with some of the ladies. When the men playing checkers laughed, Terri's heart soared.

Carol OF THE ROOMS

For the past six months, May had brought the children twice a week.

"The residents really look forward to the children's visits. Some have wonderful family support, while others have no one or limited visits. It gives them a purpose." Dani nodded toward the men.

Joe motioned to them, and they went over to stand beside him. "Thank you for suggesting the adopt-a-grandparent program," he said. "It means more than you'll ever know." His missing top tooth only added to his personality. Alexander had been taken with Bill, Joe, and some of the other men.

Terri placed a hand on his shoulder, surprised by how much she enjoyed visiting the residents and getting to know them. "It's our pleasure."

"Bring Clarence next time you come." Bill winked at her. Gramps occasionally visited with her and knew several of the men. They'd worked in ministry together in various capacities.

As with the children, the elderly here at the nursing home were the same faces Terri had seen in the rooms. Mia had quickly connected with Kathy and Lila Belle—who passed away three weeks ago.

Terri smiled at the children as they visited the older adults. When Mia rubbed her eyes, Terri knew they needed to finish up soon. The children would need a nap. She'd learned that lesson the hard way about three months earlier when Mia had a long day and had grown tired. They still had errands to run, and the seven-year-old had a breakdown in the grocery store. Terri had been both horrified and embarrassed, with no clue what to do other than to get out of there. She was not eager to repeat the incident but discovered she had more empathy for parents now when out and about.

Some of the residents at the nursing home had also voiced the need for a nap from time to time. Thirty minutes later, she motioned for Alexander to wrap up the game.

"Too bad they aren't here all the time," Joe lamented to Bill as Alexander placed the boxes on wire shelves in the storage closet.

Terri stopped folding a tablecloth and eavesdropped.

May, who held the other end of the tablecloth, gave her a quizzical look.

Terri motioned toward the men with her eyes.

"Those youngsters brighten my day," one of them said.

Terri and May shared a knowing glance. Terri's mind swirled, and she invited May to join them at Gramps's house once they left the nursing home.

Once the children were down for a nap, they sat down and brainstormed. *Is it even possible?* she wondered. Terri sketched as quickly as her hand could move. They already had plans to build a new orphanage, but now they were tweaking it. Could they make half of it a senior living center and half a children's home? She didn't know if it had ever been done or was even possible, but she was going to find out.

Somehow, I'll make it happen.

CHAPTER 34

"I don't want to leave," Mia cried one evening shortly before Christmas after spending the day with Terri and Gramps.

Terri pulled the girl into her arms, surprised she didn't want the children to leave either. "Why not?" She brushed the girl's hair behind her ear. So much had changed for all of them in the past year. She only knew these children from her visit to the rooms a year ago. Now they had captured her heart.

"It's not the same." Mia sniffed. "Ms. Patterson is good to us but—" Her little body shook with sobs. "She's not you."

When Terri wrapped the girl in her arms, love enveloped her unlike anything she'd ever felt before. She never imagined these children could capture her heart as they had. She found a nearby chair and pulled Mia onto her lap. Alexander sat at her feet. "If you could have *anything*, what would you like for Christmas?"

"To be here with you and Gramps," Mia said.

"But you visit us all the time." Were they saying what she hoped they were saying?

"No." Alexander rose on his knees. "We've talked about it." He reached for Mia's hand. "We want you to adopt us."

"You do?" Terri's eyes filled with tears. *Is this why You showed them to me in the rooms, Lord?*

"Yes. We want this to be our home."

"Will you be my mommy?" Mia wrapped her arms around Terri's neck. "We want to live with you and Gramps."

Terri peeked over at Gramps, who sat quietly observing them. Knowing her beloved grandfather, he was praying.

"This is a lot to take in." She ran a hand over Mia's hair. "I'm not going to make any promises right now, but ..." Her eyes met Alexander's. "I will think about it. And pray."

Alexander nodded. His eyes filled with hope.

"Can you give me some time?" She had to be sure. Although she couldn't imagine life without these precious children. They had enriched and blessed her life abundantly.

"Please don't take too long." Mia leaned back to look at her. "We love you."

Terri felt as if the breath had been slammed out of her. When had someone last said those words to her? When had she last been needed?

"I love you too. Both of you." Terri relished the feel of Mia as she nestled her head on her shoulder. She reached out and placed a hand on Alexander's cheek.

Have I ever said those words to anyone besides Gramps?

It felt so good to be needed and wanted. To be loved.

What do I do? Terri prayed after returning the children to the care of May Patterson.

Her mind remained deep in thought as she entered her apartment. She loved the way light shone through and couldn't believe how long she'd lived in darkness. Not just emotional darkness but physical as well. She'd purposely kept her environment and surroundings dim to match her mood. She'd missed out on so much but had no one to blame but herself for all the blessings she'd passed by. She'd been so self-centered and engrossed in making money she'd become dead inside.

Now she was truly alive. Life was much brighter and happier. She loved her apartment, but being back home, she realized how much she missed living with Gramps.

She spent a long time in prayer that evening. "I've grown to love those children."

They are yours, the voice whispered to her soul.

"Are You sure, Lord?" She couldn't help but question this promise. After all, she was forty-five years old. Past the point to safely have children of her own. But to adopt? Was she up to the challenge?

God had been showing her nothing was impossible. While she couldn't find any combined children's homes and senior living centers, it wasn't impossible. She'd spent the last two months consulting with everyone she could think of and studying the regulations.

This was different. This meant sharing her life with someone else. She'd not lived with anyone since she moved from Gramps's house after James abandoned her at the altar.

Can I share my life with someone else? Especially children?

She thought of the love Abigail had for Timmy. Watching them together touched her heart. Terri longed for that type of relationship. Her mind drifted to Timmy and how well he'd come through his surgery a few weeks earlier. He excelled in his physical therapy, and the prognosis seemed good.

Show me, Lord. She picked up her Bible, opened to Psalm 113:9, and read out loud. "He gives the barren woman a home, making her the joyous mother of children. Praise the LORD!" Terri stopped when she read the words and stared at the passage. She studied the verse repeatedly, falling asleep with those words echoing through her mind and heart.

The next morning, she woke with the children still on her mind. *Would I be a good mother? Do I even know how to be a mother?* She inhaled sharply. *I have so much to learn. I love these children. They are already the children of my heart.* Wasn't that all that mattered?

Her Bible study took her to the book of James. She opened to chapter 1, verse 17, and read aloud. "Every good gift and every perfect gift is from above, coming down from the Father of lights, with whom there is no variation or shadow due to change." She wanted to be sure before she took another step. "Lord, are You saying what I think You're saying?"

Those children are yours. The promise whispered throughout her soul again.

"Are you sure?"

Who are you to question My will?

She had her answer. At three o'clock, she surprised Abigail by telling her she'd finished for the day. Terri couldn't take it any longer. She had to get to Gramps's. The thought had weighed on her mind all day.

Terri rushed into the house, barely shutting the door. She didn't even stop to take off her coat. "What do you think of me adopting Alexander and Mia?"

Gramps sat up straight in his chair. "Tell me how you came to this conclusion."

"You know last night when Mia didn't want to leave? Well ..." She told him all about her inner struggle the night before while she took her coat off and hung it up. "I love those children. It breaks my heart every time I take them back to May." They had arranged to have them overnight for Christmas, but it would be the first time they stayed the night.

"Taking on children is an enormous commitment."

"I know." Terri paced back and forth. "I've wondered if I'm up to it. I mean, what about when I'm working?"

"They can always come here."

She stopped pacing and turned to look at him. "What if we moved in? I wouldn't worry when I'm working. You're here. Plus, Beth and Maggie are here much of the time. By the time Alexander and Mia arrive home from school, it would only be an hour or two before I'm home." That didn't include visitors such as Ethan—who now dated the nurse at work—and other friends who were often in and out. Someone else was almost always at the house with Gramps.

"You know you're welcome. I'd love to have all of you here." Gramps looked over her shoulder at the picture on the wall of her with her parents. She often caught him looking at the picture. "There's no guarantee you'll get the children."

"I know." She laughed. "I'm getting ahead of myself. As usual." She took a seat next to Gramps. "I have discussed the process with May. It's long and tedious yet so worth it."

"Can you tell me why you want the children?" Gramps studied her as if looking into her soul.

"It's easy. I love them." She would always love them. For the first time in her life, she knew what it meant to love someone wholly, not wanting anything in return. She would go to the ends of the earth for these children. *And I will always love You and be thankful, Lord.*

"About time." Gramps lifted his hands toward heaven and smiled, the familiar twinkle in his eye.

Through these children—and Gramps—God had helped her discover contentment and unconditional love.

Terri waited to tell the children about her plans to adopt them. She had no desire to get their hopes up, only to have them dashed.

After meeting with May, she visited her lawyer. She'd been pleased to discover no family waited to object or take the children back. They had been with May for three years by the time Terri filed to become their foster mom.

Once she decided to adopt them, the paperwork and wait for the children to move in felt like an eternity. In reality, it had only been a few months but seemed much longer. She'd been surprised at all that went into her being approved. For this reason, she waited until the court gave her permission before she mentioned it to the children.

"What do you think about living with me and Gramps?" She'd already moved back in with her grandfather by this point.

Mia's eyes grew wide. "You mean spend the night?"

"No. I mean live here." She motioned around the room. "With me and Gramps. You would each have your own room."

Alexander looked skeptical. "How?"

"Well ..." Terri paused a moment to calm herself. "I went before a judge and asked for you to come live with me."

Alexander scooted closer. "Because we asked you?"

"Yes." She tousled his hair. "And because I love you guys. I want to be your mommy."

"We'll be a family," Gramps said.

Mia carried her doll over to Terri. "But we don't have a daddy."

"Sometimes a family doesn't have both a mommy and a daddy." Terri pulled Mia onto her lap. "This time you'll have a mommy and a gramps. And we can be together all the time."

"Like adopted?" Mia's voice rose an octave.

"Not yet, but I'm working on it." She explained the judge gave her permission to be their foster mom, but she would have to apply to adopt them. Once the adoption process was finalized, they would be together forever, and no one could ever take them away.

Mia's eyes held a lifetime of hope. "You'll be our mommy?"

"Not at first, but hopefully soon. And then always and forever." Terri wrapped her arms around the girl. A warmth surged through her body which she'd never known before. Terri thought of her own mother, who died when she was about Mia's age, and how much she missed her. Now she and Mia would discover a mother-daughter relationship. Together.

Terri never expected the Lord would restore so much of what she had wasted. She'd lost so much in those dark and painful years. She was now choosing not to focus on the loss, but on all the exciting things ahead. The future seemed bright and the possibilities endless.

CHAPTER 35

Things accelerated over the next year, amazing Terri at how rapidly plans came together. All this had to be God's doing, she reminded herself constantly.

Three women and three men had been chosen to create a governing board over the facility, which they named Sunrise Children's Home and Senior Adult Living. Terri, serving as the seventh board member and its chairman, would make sure the facility ran according to biblical principles. Now they searched and prayed for a director. Terri had reviewed several résumés, but none appeared to be the right candidate.

"What do you think?" Terri handed Gramps the pictures she'd taken. They'd recently poured the foundation for the new facility, and she'd been excited to show him the plans manifesting into reality.

"It's huge." Gramps let out a low whistle while studying the pictures of what would be the common area. He flipped through the photos and stopped. "This is good." He held up a picture of Terri, Alexander, and Mia as they toured the facility.

She couldn't believe they were almost her children—legally. They'd been with her for six months, and she'd already filed papers for legal adoption. Now they waited for a final hearing. "I've been thinking about something, Gramps." This had been on her heart and mind for a while, but she'd not shared it with anyone but God.

Gramps tenderly stroked her cheek. "Tell me." They'd always been close but had grown even closer since her dramatic change.

"I feel God is leading me to do something more, but I'm scared."

"Of what?" He tapped his chin with his finger. She appreciated his attentiveness. Gramps always had words of wisdom and discernment.

Then she hesitated. What if this sounded as crazy to him as it did to her? "To start a ministry called Generation Outreach."

Gramps rubbed his chin. "Tell me more."

"It would build off what we're doing at Sunrise." She loved the name of the new facility. "The organization would work with children's groups and senior adult groups to bridge the generation gap. We would help facilities implement adopt-a-grandparent and adopt-a-child programs the way we have with Dani." Seeing how popular these programs had become with both age groups impressed her.

"I think it's a great idea." He bowed his head and clasped his hands. "Father, You know Terri's heart for these individuals in need. She has a great idea but concerns as well." He laid a hand on her shoulder. "What about the firm?"

"That's it. I love being an architect. I don't want to give it up." Terri reached up and covered his rough hand with hers. "I'm trying to figure out how to do both. I'd need help." At one time, she would have thought she could do it alone, but now she knew better.

"Father, show her Your will and how she can best manage her time and all these blessings You've bestowed upon her." Gramps cupped her face with his hand after he finished praying. "It will work out. You'll see."

"Do I cut back on my clients? Hire another partner?" She held up her fingers, counting off each item. "Hire someone else to establish and run Generation Outreach?" She had enough in her personal account to bankroll the start of a nonprofit.

"Well, let's talk about those options." Gramps handed her a notepad and pen from a nearby coffee table. "Could Abigail run things for you?"

"Possibly. She's returning to school now that Timmy has recovered from his surgery." Terri continued to work closely with her assistant to teach her the ins and outs of the trade. "She was so excited to receive her acceptance letter to college earlier this week." Terri could still picture her friend jumping up and down with the letter in her hand. "I think within the next three to five years she'll be a full partner."

Terri was already searching for a new administrative assistant so Abigail could move up in the firm. The new person had big shoes to fill. Abigail was so talented and came up with amazing ideas. She would make an excellent architect and partner. Terri's only regret was she didn't see the younger woman's value earlier. *I've been blind to so many things. No more. Help me see clearly, Lord. What is Your will?*

Terri and Gramps talked for hours. By the time they finished, she had a list of ideas to investigate. The project seemed doable, but figuring out the logistics would take time. Her heart felt light. She couldn't remember the last time she'd been this content.

Later that evening, Terri realized she was humming. She softly sang, "All things bright and beautiful. All creatures great and small …"

Life really is beautiful, Lord.

She'd allowed music to express her heart and soul since her transformation a few years ago, and amazement welled within at how accurately the words applied to her feelings.

"I win." Alexander beamed across the table at his opponent.

"You got me again." Clarence Neely forced himself to pout. He loved having these children in the house.

Maggie entered the den where he spent most of his time. "You have company."

Clarence had never been happier. Terri and her aunts had renewed the closeness of childhood. Things weren't always easy, but they kept working on their attitudes and relationships. The peace he'd prayed for over the years had finally been fulfilled. It tickled him God had allowed him to live long enough to see this reconciliation.

He looked up from the checkerboard. "Who is it?"

Maggie gave him a huge grin. "You'll see."

"We'll play another game later," he said to Alexander.

Alexander scooted out of the room.

Clarence Neely didn't know what to expect, but he smiled as a man appeared in the doorway. Time had been good to his friend. He'd stayed in shape and looked the same, except for the white hair creeping in along his temples. "You remind me of a young man I once knew." Clarence forced himself up with the help of his walker.

The man stood before him in an expensive black suit, brightened only by a white pocket square. "It's been a long time, sir."

Carol OF THE ROOMS

His old friend stepped forward with an extended hand. Instead, Clarence drew him into a bear hug. Then he stepped back for a better view. "Mark Beaver. Let me look at you." He patted the man's shoulder. "It's good to see you, son."

"You too, old man." Warmth filled Mark's eyes and smile.

"This is a surprise. What are you doing here?"

Both men took a seat.

"I'm hoping to move back to the area."

"How's the family?"

Mark told him about his children—two boys and two girls. They were busy with school and a variety of extracurricular activities.

Clarence wanted to know more. "And your wife?"

A shadow crossed over Mark's eyes. He stared at his hands. "She died. Car accident."

Listening to the details, Clarence realized she'd perished in an accident similar to the one Terri had survived. Ironically—or maybe not so ironically—if he understood correctly, the accidents happened around the same time. Could it really have been three years ago?

Mark broke down as he shared. He wanted to relocate back to Charlotte so he'd be closer to his parents. They had recently retired, and he wanted to enjoy these years with them. They would also help with his children.

"I hope you will move back." Clarence would love to see more of Mark. Too much time had passed since their last visit.

"That's definitely the plan." Mark had an assurance about him. He'd always possessed this trait, but maturity had honed it.

"Terri said she saw you on the news several years ago." Clarence watched for any hint of emotion from the younger man at the mention of his granddaughter.

"Yes, I come to town occasionally on business matters. We also come to visit my parents as often as possible." Mark sat up straighter. He looked over Clarence's shoulder. "It'll do us good to start over. I can't think of any place better to live than near my parents." An easy smile came over his face. "Besides, I've missed you."

Clarence would enjoy seeing the young man on a regular basis. "It's been too long. What do you do now?" The last he'd heard, Mark taught at a business school. *Hmmm ... how long ago was that?*

"I've been an administrator at a nursing home for over a decade." A slow smile crossed his face. "I interviewed a few hours ago for a new facility. I love the unusual concept."

Clarence's jaw dropped. *What are You up to, Lord?* He felt his heart skip a beat. *It couldn't be. Could it?* "What's the name of the facility?" His voice had grown raspy.

"Sunrise."

Clarence closed his eyes. *Thank You, Lord.* In his gut, he knew the board had found their director. What would Terri say about this latest development? Clearly, she'd not seen his résumé, or she would have mentioned it. It surprised him she'd not been aware of Mark's candidacy. Initially, she'd been involved in the hiring process, but it took more time than she'd been able to donate. Particularly when she began designing a huge project for Ray Peterson. Terri would have final approval, though, over whomever the board chose as their administrator.

Clarence couldn't wait to see the face of both his granddaughter and Mark when they discovered the other's involvement with Sunrise. This could only be the work of one person—the Lord. Clarence Neely smiled to himself. *Is this all part of Your plan?* He knew the answer in his soul, and peace overcame him. Time would tell if his hunches held merit.

Mark looked over his head at the pictures of Terri on the wall.

Recently, Clarence had his daughters add a picture of Terri with Mia and Alexander to the collection. His favorite, though, was the one of Terri with Maggie and Beth. It was underneath a picture of the three of them taken shortly before her parents' death. The past and the present.

He waited patiently for Mark to bring up the subject. He'd learned long ago some subjects couldn't be rushed.

Mark told him about his work, anecdotes about his children, and what he would miss about where they lived when they returned to Charlotte. "It'll be good to be back home. I've missed living here." He motioned with his hands as his eyes flew once again to the pictures of Terri. "A lot of wonderful memories."

Clarence looked at the pictures. "I remember when you taught her to defend herself." He grinned at the younger man. "Took her a while to get the hang of it."

Mark laughed. "As I recall, she didn't make it easy on me." A serious look came over his face, and his eyes searched the room. They sat in silence before Mark blew out a long breath. "How is she?" His voice wavered for the first time.

Clarence couldn't blame the man for being leery. The answer would have been vastly different three short years ago.

"Why don't you ask her yourself?" a soft voice answered from the doorway.

Clarence hadn't heard his granddaughter arrive home. Had she been standing there eavesdropping all this time? That wasn't her way. Then again, this was Mark Beaver.

From the light in both their eyes, Clarence knew life would never be the same. The two moved as one to embrace.

Time stood still as they laughed and joked together throughout the remainder of the evening. Time picked up where it left off so long ago.

Later that night, he heard Terri singing in the other room. "I sing because I'm happy. I sing because I'm free."

He added his own baritone voice to her beautiful soprano. "For his eye is on the sparrow. And I know He watches me."

EPILOGUE

"You look pleased."

Gabriel glanced up from the scene before him as Sandalphon, his fellow archangel, approached. "I am. Just came from a wedding." Gabriel's heart overflowed with happiness over the latest turn of events.

Sandalphon raised an eyebrow. "Really? Whose?"

Gabriel laughed. "Like you don't know." It had taken this archangel of music working steadily behind the scenes with his songs and colors to turn things around for Terri Neely. This beautiful wedding had been the result of his handiwork.

"Humor me."

Gabriel laughed again, happy to oblige. "Mark Beaver and Terri Neely." He reached through time and space to pluck a purple lilac from the altar flowers.

Sandalphon clapped his hands together, and a song filled the air. "It's about time." One thing was for sure. Wherever he was, music would be too.

"I couldn't agree more." Amazement filled Gabriel at all the details only God could orchestrate. Then again, God was the master of the universe. The angels had seen Him perform innumerable miracles throughout the ages. Why were they still surprised every time?

Sandalphon pulled up a seat. "So, catch me up."

"Terri adopted a third child about a year ago, around the time she reconnected with Mark. Today, they have combined their families, with seven children between them. We already have a dog who will soon join their family." Gabriel reached up, and the scene unfolded. "Gramps predicted correctly Mark would become the new director of Sunrise."

"Wonderful. And everyone else?"

They peeked in on Abigail, who had one more year left in college. "Terri promised her a partnership upon completion. The two women will become the top architectural team in the Southeast. Timmy is thriving after his surgery and has a long life ahead of him." The scene fast-forwarded. "As you can see, Timmy will become a lawyer and head Generation Outreach in due time."

Sandalphon nodded, and the scene returned to the present.

"Terri has been as good as her word in helping others. She is transformed, and everyone who knew her before the accident still marvels at the change. Time and again, she shares her testimony with anyone who will listen. She stays busy with her firm, Sunrise, and Generation Outreach, but always makes it a point to put God and family first," Gabriel said proudly.

"Good to hear."

"She appointed a director to Generation Outreach and sits in on planning meetings. Terri became inspired to introduce a creative arts program and to partner with animal shelters, bringing animals into the business plan for Generation Outreach. The administrative team at Sunrise is piloting and integrating this program, which will continue to spread throughout the United States." Then Gabriel made a prediction. "I'd say within a few years, the program will expand internationally."

The two angels watched as the scene shifted to Ethan, who married the nurse he'd been dating. Amazingly, they became good friends with Terri and Mark. Ethan was appointed as the director of nursing at Sunrise.

Next, they visited Clarence Neely, who was sad to see his granddaughter and her children leave his home. Yet he was overjoyed because Terri and Mark were finally married. From the moment the two saw one another that afternoon, the outcome had been obvious. The timing finally worked out for them to be together.

"I'm a happy man," Gramps said, adjusting his bowtie for the reception. "I've seen all I longed to see accomplished in this full life of mine. Officiating the wedding of my granddaughter and Mark will completely fulfill my prayers for this life."

Gabriel smiled as he listened to the older man hum a song. "Terri and Gramps are a lot alike."

Sandalphon beamed. "And beautiful music has become the soundtrack of Terri Neely Beaver's soul."

"Thanks to you."

"Music has an amazing effect on the heart. Besides, I wasn't alone."

Gabriel nodded. "We'll have to be sure to thank Charles for letting us borrow the gift the Lord gave him."

"He had his own special song." Sandalphon hummed the author's tune. He loved using his music to change and shape others. "Bless good old Dickens."

"While we wait for Charlie, let's peek in on Terri one more time." Gabriel waited with excitement as the scene morphed again. It was morning time.

Sandalphon grinned. "I wonder what she's singing now?"

As Terri prepared a pot of coffee, she sang. Her soul sang with her in both word and spirit as she lifted her praise to God.

Gabriel and Sandalphon couldn't resist joining in. They turned toward the Lord and added their voices to Terri's. The song rose in their own souls near the end of the verse. The archangels bent in worship as together they reached the end: "How Great Thou Art!"

AUTHOR NOTES

Dear Readers,

Thank you for taking the time to read Terri's story. I pray it touched and inspired you as much as it did me in writing the story.

Music has always been an integral part of my life, but like Terri, I've had a love-hate relationship with it at times and have had to work through my feelings and learn to come to terms with this complex relationship.

In this day and age, it seems difficult to picture an orphanage in such dire straits or structured in such a manner in the United States as the one May ran. At least, the optimistic part of me hopes none are in such dreadful situations. To keep the story parallel to the traditional *A Christmas Carol*, I presented that aspect of the story in a manner that sticks closer to the Dickens version as the themes of want and ignorance were so important to him. This decision also allowed me to provide the orphans with a hopeful and unique ending.

Another aspect where I took inspiration from Dickens is in Timmy's story. Research shows a child with cerebral palsy could learn to walk with surgery, a fact which made it plausible to parallel Dickens's character Tiny Tim using this ailment for Timmy. Later on, I met my dear friend Theresa Patten, a mom of a child with cerebral palsy, who provided me invaluable feedback on Timmy's character.

Today, charities and some children's hospitals may be able to provide free of charge a crucial surgery like Timmy needed, but I chose not to explore that option to stay true to the original version. Also, Timmy's potential death may seem extreme to some, but research shows death is a possibility for severe cases of cerebral palsy. So for that section, I went with the worst of the worst scenarios.

Finally, I've worked in nursing homes in a variety of ways for over a decade. My research has never turned up a half-nursing home, half-orphanage structured the way I created Sunrise, although I have seen daycares within nursing homes. Yet I love the idea of one day seeing a real-life Sunrise.

Having worked as an activity director and now a certified activity consultant for so long, I've seen firsthand the way nursing home residents will light up and their moods improve when children are around. Maybe one day, someone will take the initiative to create such an intergenerational, dual-facility endeavor. I think it would be a challenge but an ultimate success for everyone involved.

If your heart has been burdened for orphans and/or senior adults, please reach out to local organizations in your area to determine how you can volunteer or help out.

I love to connect with my readers. Please take a moment to follow me on social media or, for more information, stop by my website at DianaLeaghMatthews.com and follow my newsletter for the most up-to-date news. If you are part of a book club, I also have a book club kit available on my website and would love to talk with you.

Until next time, keep your eyes above,

Leagh

ABOUT THE AUTHOR

Diana Leagh Matthews has a heart for the hurting and shares God's love through her story from rebel to redeemed. She has a bachelor's degree in music and has worked in the healthcare industry in non-clinical roles for the past decade. Leagh (pronounced L-e-e) is a speaker, vocalist, teacher, genealogist, and presents historical and Biblical monologues. *Carol of the Rooms* is her debut novel, and she has a series of Breath Prayer books also available. She lives in South Carolina with her spunky Maltese. For more information or to check out her stories behind the hymns visit her at <u>DianaLeaghMatthews.com</u>.

BOOK CLUB QUESTIONS

1. Terri and Marlee lived by the motto money is the only thing that matters. Why do you think this belief has infiltrated our society?

2. Terri retaliated if anyone went against her wishes. Have you known anyone like this? How did you handle the situation? Would you have done anything differently?

3. Even though Terri hardened her heart, Gramps remained a soft spot. Why do you think that was? How did Ethan begin to broach that barrier?

4. How does Terri's relationship with music express her current heart condition?

5. Gramps and Ethan discuss Saul/Paul's Damascus Road experience. Do you think such experiences are still possible today? Is this what Terri experienced?

6. Gramps prayed for Terri for years. Is there someone you've prayed for a long time? Do you continue to hold onto hope, or does the situation feel helpless? Why or why not?

7. Terri prided herself on being self-reliant and strong. Yet in her moment of need, she cried out to God for help. Why do you think we (the human race) feel we can treat our relationship with God as a yo-yo, to come and go at will?

8. What would the soundtrack of your life reveal about you? How has your soundtrack changed over the years? What songs make up the soundtrack of your life?

9. Terri has the unique opportunity to view her life—her past, present, and future. Would you want to relive your life? Would you want to see your future? Why or why not?

10. Terri allowed hurt and humiliation to rule her life. She shut down her feelings. Do you shut down when hurt? How do you find the strength to bounce back?

11. Was Mark wrong to give up on Terri? Why or why not? Have you waited or longed for something, and it never happened or took years to reach fruition? Did you ever give up hope?

12. Terri is allowed to see her alternate reality and how different choices would have affected her life. If God permitted it, would you want to see your alternate reality? Why or why not?

13. Why do you think the spirit took her to an orphanage and nursing home? How did these locations relate to Terri's present life? How did she help these individuals after her experience in the rooms of her life?

14. Terri had a lot of apologies to make. Is there someone you need to forgive or apologize to? Is there someone you wished would forgive you?

15. Terri told herself a lot of lies over the years and believed the lies others told her about herself. How do you see yourself? What lies have others told you that you believed?

16. How have you been broken and spilled out? Where were you once blind but now you can see?

17. Do you blame Ethan for not accepting a second chance to be with Terri? Were you surprised they became friends later on?

18. Whom do you relate most with in your walk with Jesus? An angry Terri? A genie-wishing Victoria Nelson? A hopeful May Patterson? Or a believing Gramps? Why?

19. James 1:27 tells us to care for the widows and orphans. How can you help today's widows and orphans in your area?

20. Who has taught you how to love unconditionally? What relationships have required some work?

21. Terri struggled to know if she was in God's will. Tell of a time you ran ahead of God. Tell of a time you questioned and dragged your feet. How did God meet you in each place?

22. How has the Lord restored things previously lost in your life?

23. Has God called you to do something that scared you? What was it? What did you do?

24. Have you experienced a situation or event in your life only the Lord could have orchestrated?

25. How has prayer changed your life? How has praying for others changed their lives?

DISCOVER YOUR LIFE'S SOUNDTRACK

What type of soundtrack does your life have? Take the quiz:

www.discoverthesoundtrackofourlives.com

COMING SPRING 2024

FOREVER CHANGED

PROLOGUE

APRIL 2015
NEW YORK CITY

Everything was about to change. Danielle Davis could feel it as she stepped off the stage, peering through the curtains as the house lights came up. People bustled about backstage, energizing her. She had given a Tony-award performance in her first leading role on Broadway. *The Magical Castle* was a new musical she'd workshopped for two years. Danielle knew in her soul she would reach the fame she desired with this role. This show would do for her what *Wicked* had done for Kristin Chenoweth and Idina Menzel.

All her dreams were about to come true. All the hard work of the past decade had begun to pay off. No longer would she be a C-list actor. She was on her way to becoming a star. Over the years, she'd had moderate success on the small screen, but her dream had always been to make it on Broadway. After years of struggling, the time had finally arrived.

"Fabulous." Joel, her boyfriend of two years, pulled her into his arms for a passionate kiss the moment she stepped from the stage. She was breathless by the time he stepped back and handed her a bouquet of roses. Joel kept his tradition of presenting her with flowers on opening night.

Allison, her assistant, wedged her way between them. "Danielle." She grabbed Danielle's hand and pulled her through the throng of people gathered backstage. Once they reached her dressing room, Allison's face turned a ghostly white.

Danielle wasn't sure whether to be angry or bewildered by Allison's damper on her celebration. "What's going on?"

"Your sister—"

Danielle held up her hand. While she'd refused her sister's call several hours ago, they had just spoken yesterday.

Meghan had tried to call her again today, as was her opening-night tradition, but Danielle had ignored the call.

Danielle cringed at the memory. She and Joel were sitting on her couch kissing. When she hit the ignore button, she leaned back and pulled Joel with her. He'd really helped get her heart rate up.

"Listen to me." Allison's voice was so forceful Danielle stared at her. The girl was usually quiet, and Danielle had never heard her so commanding.

"What is going on in here?" Joel barged into the dressing room. "How dare you—" He turned on Allison.

"Shut up." Allison didn't even bother to look at him. "You need to listen to me." Allison held Danielle's gaze, but all Danielle could feel was the squeeze of Joel's hand on hers. He was ready to go.

Danielle turned to follow Joel. "I'll call her tomorrow."

Allison rushed to the dressing room door and barricaded it with her body.

"You need to listen to me. Now." She hissed.

Apparently, this was pretty serious. "What?" Danielle tapped her foot impatiently and crossed her arms.

"You need to call home." Allison's eyes darkened, and her voice became taut.

FOREVER CHANGED

"I told you I would tomorrow." Danielle sighed in irritation. *What was so important?*

Allison pulled a cellphone from her pocket and held it out. "Now."

"Get out of our way." Joel wasn't in the mood for these games. No surprise there.

"Wait." Danielle wasn't sure what made her speak. Sorrow filled Allison's face.

Something was wrong. Danielle knew it in her gut. She'd been through this moment once before. When her whole life changed, she ran to New York to pursue her dream.

As she looked in Allison's eyes, something told her everything was about to change. Again. She feared it wasn't in the good way she'd envisioned when she stepped off the stage. *Had that only been moments ago?*

"What's wrong?" She could barely get the words out for the fear building inside.

"There's been an accident."

Danielle reached behind her for a chair but couldn't find it.

Joel guided her to the nearby sofa.

"Who?" She didn't want to hear this. She'd lost so much already.

"Trevor and Meghan."

"What? No." She shook her head. It couldn't be. *There had to be a mistake.*

"They were in the lake, and the current sucked them under."

Allison refused to meet her eyes.

"They're gone?" Danielle leaned into the sofa. She wanted to cry or scream or something. Her body tensed, but no sound came.

"Divers found both bodies several hours later."

"The kids?" *They did everything as a family. The kids had to be with them.*

"A neighbor had them. Offered to give Meghan and Trevor a brief respite."

The room spun. She struggled to breathe. Danielle gasped but couldn't fill her lungs with air. *Is this what dying felt like?*

"What—" She couldn't get the words out. The room continued to spin. In an instant, everything changed.

One tragedy had sent her running. Another pulled her back.

It was too much. She couldn't deal with it.

The room spun faster now. She couldn't catch her breath as her heart pounded. Then everything went dark.

CHAPTER 1

Caleb Donovan leaned against the wall and held up a sign with a name on it. He watched the luggage turn round and round on the conveyor belt. His best friends were gone. *How had this happened?* Caleb would never forget pulling their bodies out of the water after the accident. Upon receiving the phone call, he had been one of the first to arrive at the lake to assist with the recovery efforts. A lump formed in his throat. Everything felt so uncertain now. After licking his wounds for years, the time had finally come to return to his passion for music. His manager wasn't thrilled when he canceled his upcoming tour dates, but he couldn't leave. Not now.

He had so much to consider. He stared at the passengers making their way to the luggage rack.

A woman caught his eye. She held her head high, but her eyes looked red. He assumed she was in her early-to-mid-thirties, around his age. She wore an expensive designer dress, and her auburn hair flowed down her back. *Way too much makeup.* In his mind, she should be on a magazine cover.

She stopped to stare at her reflection in the mirror and patted her hair.

Stepping forward, he held up the sign. "Danielle Davis?"

A child bumped into her. She jumped back and rolled her eyes. "Yes." She plastered on a smile and gripped her suitcase handle.

"I'm Caleb Donovan. Trevor and I were best friends." He could still see his friend atop a horse, pushing back his cowboy hat. Trevor had a way of commanding his horse, and his muscular build allowed him to easily command the cows and other animals on the farm. "Welcome back to South Carolina. I'm so sorry for your loss."

She spun around. "That's nice. I need my luggage."

Caleb grunted and helped her pull the indicated suitcases from the conveyor belt. With her baggage in tow, she followed him to his truck.

It was going to be a long drive if she ignored him for the hour-long ride.

"Is there anything I can answer for you?" According to Meghan, her sister had never returned home once she left for New York City.

She inspected her acrylic nails. "How long should I expect to stay?"

Caleb gripped the steering wheel. "Meghan and Trevor's lawyer can answer that better. I took the liberty of setting up a meeting for tomorrow afternoon."

Danielle nodded but never looked in his direction.

"Trevor was my best friend. Anything I can do to be of assistance?"

"No. Thank you." She looked at her phone before turning it over. "How much further?"

Caleb kept his eyes on the road. "About forty minutes."

She sighed and turned to look out the window at the mixture of trees and homes scattered along the highway.

Caleb tried several times on the ride to engage her, but she ignored him. *Why had Meghan left the kids to this*

FOREVER CHANGED

woman's care? At least, that was what everyone assumed had been set up. He vaguely remembered a conversation six months ago in that regard. He looked at Danielle out of the corner of his eye. *She won't last a week.* If he were a betting man, he'd be willing to take bets. She would be overwhelmed with country life. The question was, what would happen to the children then?

Several neighborhood ladies would help, and he'd do all he could, but eventually they'd all have to find a new norm.

How could two sisters be so different? She had no clue what was in store for her.

The last day had been a whirlwind of planning to leave New York and travel to the small town of Ninety Six, South Carolina.

Danielle saw, without seeing, the sights as they whirled by. The trees out to her sister's farm sped past in a blur. She couldn't believe her sister was gone. The emotions overwhelmed her.

She'd never wanted to return to her hometown. Now, here she was.

Before she could think through one clear sentence, the car stopped, and her door opened. Some things never changed. Even after almost two decades. The house looked the same as when she'd run away all those years ago.

"This way." Caleb, the local farmer who chauffeured her, nodded toward the house. She shook her head, unable to speak.

Danielle stretched out her long legs, and her high heels landed in a water puddle. A string of words that would have caused her mama to wash her mouth out with soap poured forth.

Her eyes watered, and she blinked her heavily mascaraed eyelashes several times.

The man handed her a handkerchief. "You'll get through this."

She'd not seen a real white handkerchief in years. Clearly, he thought she was upset over her sister's untimely death, but those tears had come at the remembrance of her mama.

Danielle found her footing and followed the man into her sister's home.

The door barely opened before she longed to turn and run.

Caleb positioned his body to block her escape.

She stood in the doorway and blinked, allowing her eyes to adjust to the scene as a baby screamed. The child must be behind the closed door in the far-left corner.

A young child, maybe two years old—but she couldn't be sure—ran around with wild abandon.

"Liam. Come here."

Danielle followed the voice and recognized the face of her oldest niece. She'd not seen the girl since she was a young child, but her sister had regularly sent pictures. Not that she'd paid a lot of attention. Meghan's chatter about her children had always seemed endless.

Now they are orphans.

Liam walked over to the oldest girl, who pulled him onto her lap and whispered something in his ear. Danielle watched a moment before allowing her eyes to travel down to the couch. Sitting side by side were an abundance of children. All looked morose. The girls wore dresses, and the boys had on khakis and freshly pressed shirts.

"Welcome." A woman in slacks and an apron stepped

out of the kitchen on the right and wiped her hands on a dish towel. "You must be Danielle."

Danielle nodded. The man standing behind her pushed her gently forward.

"This is—" Caleb wrapped an arm around the older woman's shoulders.

"Where's my room?" Danielle needed a moment to calm her nerves and wrap her mind around being back here.

"Children." The woman turned and motioned toward them on the couch. "This is your Aunt Danielle." They gawked at her the same way she stared at them.

Danielle counted. One ... two ... three. There were so many of them. Four ... five. *Was my sister crazy?* Six children.

A door opened. A younger woman in jeans carried the baby and placed her on the couch with the other children. Seven children?

Danielle crossed her arms. She had always wondered why Meghan had so many.

"I'll show you where you can put your belongings." Caleb led the way. "Are you okay?" He spoke through gritted teeth once they reached the hallway.

She couldn't meet his gaze. *Was she okay? What a silly question.* Her sister was gone, and she'd been forced to return to the one place she never wanted to see again.

Caleb opened the door to reveal a small room. A single bed had been pushed against the wall with a nightstand beside it. At the foot of the bed was a dresser, and a small desk stood in the opposite corner.

She had to suppress a laugh at how small the closet was. Her bathroom in New York City was three times the size. Where would she put everything she brought? Not knowing how long she'd be here, half her wardrobe ended up in her suitcase.

"You'll want to change into something more

comfortable." With his pronouncement, Caleb closed the door.

Thankful to finally be alone, Danielle flung herself across the bed and allowed the sobs she'd kept inside, along with the shudders that accompanied them, to escape. Burying her head in the homemade quilt, she let the tears come. Joel had been uncomfortable with her crying. He'd finally left last night because he couldn't handle her grief.

Danielle wasn't sure how much time passed before she slowly gathered herself together. She'd rather be anywhere but here. Somehow, she had to get through this. She went through her suitcase and decided on a pair of designer jeans and a cream-colored blouse.

Taking a deep breath, she left her room and went into the kitchen. An older woman with long hair which fell around her shoulders sat at the table with Play-Doh. The woman who greeted her when she arrived stood beside the counter preparing sandwiches.

"Glad to see you. Come help me." The woman fixing the food gave her a reassuring smile and pointed toward a bag of chips on top of the refrigerator.

Danielle busied herself by grabbing the nearby chips and adding a handful to each plate.

"I'm Dee Dee, by the way. I live across the road." She had her hair pulled back in a knot at her neck. The sweater she wore and the scarf around her neck gave her a classic look.

Danielle nodded. "Nice to meet you." She looked down at her hands. "You already know I'm Danielle." She really should apologize for her rudeness earlier but couldn't figure out where to begin.

"How long since you talked to your sister?" Dee Dee stuck the knife into the peanut butter and pulled it out for another swipe across the bread.

FOREVER CHANGED

Danielle moved to the next plate and added more chips. "The day before she died."

"Did she tell you anything about her life?" Dee Dee handed her a completed sandwich to be served.

"Some."

"Do you know anything about your sister's life?" Dee Dee turned to look at her as she repeated the question, and Danielle felt as if she saw through her.

Danielle wished she'd paid better attention. "Only what she told me."

"But did you hear what she was saying?" Dee Dee had deep blue eyes which seemed to see into her soul.

Danielle knew the woman understood she had no idea what she'd walked into. Danielle stared blankly back.

"I didn't think so." Dee Dee sighed as she reached for a hand towel to wipe her hands.

A banging began on the table. Danielle jumped and turned to the older woman at the kitchen table. She had thin, dirty-blond hair with gray streaks, but something about her looked familiar.

Danielle turned back toward Dee Dee. "Who is she?"

Dee Dee gave her a curious look. "Don't you know?"

Danielle shook her head.

Instead of answering her question, Dee Dee walked over to the kitchen table, pulled out a chair, and sat beside the woman. "Hi, Caroline." Dee Dee spoke soothingly.

The other woman looked up, and Danielle gasped. *It couldn't be. Could it?*

"Are you playing us a tune?" Dee Dee nodded toward the utensils as if she had all the time in the world.

Caroline nodded.

"I like it. Do you recognize our friend?"

Caroline looked at Danielle and nodded again as her

eyes widened.

"Who is she?" Dee Dee picked up Caroline's hand.

"Mary Jane." The woman's voice was barely more than a whisper. Her grandmother may have mistaken Danielle for her mama, but Danielle definitely recognized this strange woman sitting before her.

Danielle blinked, struggling to understand what happened.

Her grandmother had always been so full of life.

Danielle waited until Dee Dee moved into the laundry room and threw another load of clothes into the dryer. "What's wrong with her?"

"She has dementia." Dee Dee handed her a basket, which she filled with dry towels. "She probably has Alzheimer's."

"Her voice is so weak." Danielle didn't understand any of this. She'd heard her sister mention their grandmother but never realized how bad her condition had become. It had been fifteen years since she'd been home. In her mind, her grandmother was still a vibrant, outgoing woman. Not the shell of a person who sat before her a moment ago. *How could this have happened to her?*

Danielle pulled Dee Dee over to the side, not wanting to be overheard. "What happened?"

"As I told you, she has dementia." Dee Dee covered her hands with her own. "You've much to learn."

Danielle's eyes slammed shut. She didn't want to learn or even be here. Forcing herself to focus on the situation at hand, she thought of her grandmother. "Why is her voice so weak?"

"That's because she seldom talks." Dee Dee started the dryer. And pointed for her to carry the basket to the living room.

"So, how do I understand what she needs?" Danielle did as directed and set the basket on a now-empty couch.

She should ask where the children were but wasn't ready to. Not yet.

Dee Dee gave her a reassuring smile, which put her at ease. "You'll learn."

Danielle grabbed her arm. "But how?"

Dee Dee laid a hand over Danielle's. "By the light in her eyes and the expressions on her face."

"This is all too much." She ran her other hand through her long tresses. A heavy weight settled on her shoulders.

Things couldn't get any worse. Or could they?

The noise around the kitchen table was mind-boggling. Danielle wanted to join the baby when she screamed. She was not used to so much noise.

"Follow me." Dee Dee motioned with her finger.

Danielle followed her into a back bedroom next to the one she'd been shown to before.

"Look who the tide dragged in." An old woman sat against a pile of pillows. "Don't recognize me, eh?" The woman's laugh sounded more like a cackle. "Always wanted to make a name for yerself. How did you do in the Apple?"

Danielle shook her head at the woman's ignorance. "You mean the Big Apple?"

The woman's green eyes twinkled as if they held some secret. "Did you make it as a canary?"

"What?" Danielle had no idea what this woman was saying. The words coming out of her mouth were English, but everything else was completely foreign.

"I see we have some educatin' to do."

"I'm not dumb. I have a college deg—" Danielle's back straightened.

"I didn't say you were dumb. Only we need to talk the same language." The woman pulled herself up in the bed, and Dee Dee fluffed her pillows and placed them behind her back.

Danielle took a step closer. "Who are you?" Something seemed familiar, but she couldn't place it. Not yet.

"I told you she wouldn't know." The woman turned to Dee Dee with a mischievous twinkle in her eyes. She turned back to Danielle. "My name is Rachel Emma Timmerman Harling Taylors."

She flashed a wide, toothless grin at the younger girl.

Danielle coughed. *Could this day get any weirder?* "My great-grandmother?" Danielle swore the old woman died years ago. After all, she'd already been old by the time Danielle was a teenager. *Am I talking to a ghost?*

"One and the same." The old woman smiled like a Cheshire cat and looked like she'd eaten a canary.

"You can't be." Her voice rose two octaves. Danielle let out a long breath.

The woman patted the blanket covering her legs. "And why not?"

"Because—you must be at least a hundred years old."

"I'll be one hundred October 16. I got another good six months, so donna rush me."

Danielle sank into the rocker in the corner.

"So let me see if I understand. My sister and her husband had—" She had to stop and think for a moment. "Seven children, took care of our grandmother—who has Alzheimer's—and—" Danielle stared at the woman lying in the bed. "Cared for our hundred-year-old great-grandmother?"

"Almost one hundred. Don't rush me yet. I'm still a

spring chicken. I'm not ready to be over the hill—yet. Otherwise—you're hotsy totsy." Her great-grandmother leaned her head back against her pillow as long white hair cascaded down.

Danielle leaned over with her hands on her thighs. Her lungs felt empty. "Why didn't you tell me?" She shot the accusation toward Dee Dee.

Dee Dee helped her back to her feet. "We thought you knew. At least some of it."

Danielle leaned against the doorway and closed her eyes. She was barely responsible for herself. How could she ever be responsible for nine other people? *How am I going to support all of them? My career is in New York City, not here.*

No way she could ever afford a flat for ten people.

Well, eleven—if Joel didn't completely run the other way.

Maybe she could put her grandmother and great-grandmother in a nursing home. But what about the children? She'd heard stories growing up of families farming children out. Did they have neighbors willing to take them? Did people still do that today?

As she contemplated the possibility—one that sounded really good to her—she knew this was the last thing her sister would want. Meghan was a saint. Danielle did not know how she did it.

Her mind spun a thousand different directions.

The responsibility. She couldn't do this.

What was she going to do? How fast could she get out of here?

She struggled for a breath. Then another one. Then she jumped from her seat and bolted from the room.

Danielle could have sworn her great-grandmother spoke but had no idea what she said. She had to get away, and no one was going to stop her. Returning to the kitchen, a multitude of eyes fell on her. She looked around until the patio beckoned her. Without stopping, she marched over and slammed the back door.

Running into the yard, she stopped, leaned over, and supported her hands on her knees as she tried to catch a wind of breath. Breathe in. Deep breathe. Fresh air. She needed air.

Looking around, she couldn't believe the sight.

Five dogs of all different sizes and shapes ran around apple trees across the field. To the left were free-roaming chickens and coops. Then there were pigs, cows, sheep, horses. Was that a mule? Moving around, she saw a beehive and, further on, a pen of rabbits.

When they'd driven in, she'd paid no attention to any of the details or surroundings. Land stretched as far as her eye could see. Over half the farmland lay covered in hay bales. *When is the last time I saw a hay bale?* Some areas had a grove of trees, gardens, or animal pens, while other places were nothing more than rolling hills or a forest area. If she were in a better mindset, the land would be beautiful.

I'm a city girl. Not a farm girl.

Danielle thought she'd stepped back in time into a scene from *Little House on the Prairie*. Except, this was ten times worse than even that popular TV show she had once enjoyed.

She felt another panic attack rising and turned to look at all the pens and land, a sight which made her dizzy. Overwhelmed. It all overwhelmed her.

What do I do now?

This is not my life. She and her sister had always been different, but Danielle had never considered how different.

FOREVER CHANGED

The last thing she ever wanted was a family and the dream of happily ever after. Meanwhile, Meghan's greatest dream had been to be a wife and mother.

Danielle walked toward a grove of trees that stood alone.

As she moved closer to the nearby pond, the ducks approached the edge.

She sank onto a fallen log and looked out over the water.

The scene was beautiful, even a little soothing.

Something moved across the bottom of her leg. Danielle looked down and let out a blood-curdling scream.

Made in the USA
Columbia, SC
12 March 2024

32561138R00137